SPIRITS WITHIN

A Haunted Anthology

K.A. MORSE   SAMANTHA BEA
STEPHANIE HASSENPLUG   JENÉE ROBINSON
C.L. THORNTON   ALEXIS TAYLOR   EVELYN BELLE

Rinna, don't forget to sleep with your night light on.

Illustrated by
EVE GRAPHIC DESIGN LLC.

Copyright © 2021
K.A. Morse, Samantha Bea, Stephanie Hassenplug, Jenée Robinson, C.L. Thornton, Alexis, Taylor, & Evelyn Belle.
This is a work of fiction. Names, characters, places, and incidents either are the products of the author's imagination or are used fictitiously. Any resemblance to actual persons, living or dead, businesses, companies, events, or locales is entirely coincidental.
All Rights Reserved. No part of this book may be reproduced or used in any manner without the express written permission of the publisher except for the use of brief quotations in a book review.
This eBook is licensed for your personal enjoyment only. This eBook may not be re-sold or given away to other people. If you would like to share this book with another person, please purchase an additional copy for each recipient.

| About Stephanie Hassenplug | 113 |
| Other books by Stephanie Hassenplug: | 115 |

Specter's Inc.

Chapter 1	121
Chapter 2	127
Chapter 3	133
Chapter 4	141
Chapter 5	150
About the Author	153
Also By Jenée Robinson	155

Making Friends

Chapter 1	161
Chapter 2	166
Chapter 3	169
Chapter 4	174
Chapter 5	178
Chapter 6	181
Acknowledgments and Thank Yous	185

Necro: A Rejected Mates Prequel

Chapter 1	191
Chapter 2	195
Chapter 3	199
Chapter 4	203
Chapter 5	205
Chapter 6	209
Chapter 7	216
Alexis Taylor	219
Other Books by Alexis Taylor	221
Shorts and anthology stories	223

Contents

Drina

Chapter 1	5
Chapter 2	10
Chapter 3	15
Chapter 4	18
Chapter 5	21
Chapter 6	28
Chapter 7	34
Chapter 8	38
About K.A. Morse	45
Also By K.A. Morse	47

Claimed

Author's Note	53
Chapter 1	55
Chapter 2	58
Chapter 3	64
Chapter 4	69
About Samantha Bea	73
Samantha Bea's Links	75
Also by Samantha Bea	77

Unwanted Attachments

Chapter 1	83
Chapter 2	93
Chapter 3	101
Chapter 4	106

This book is dedicated to Veterans everywhere. They risked it all so we could have it all.

Haunted Kind Of Love

Chapter 1 — 229
About Evelyn Belle — 279

Drina

BY: K.A MORSE

Ghost Level

To my Best friend Drina. I love you always.

Chapter One

GRAMP'S PLACE

The drive to our new home felt longer than I thought. I get out of the truck stretching my legs as I do, the crisp morning air hitting my face. I breathe it in. You can't get this kind of fresh air in the city. Meko did most of the driving as I slept. Long drives always make me sleepy. Bandit zooms out of the truck to check out the land, silly dog. This house is not something I remember much of, but my grandpa left it to me in his will. Our homestead sits on about ten acres, surrounded by farmland. Gramps wasn't a great farmer, so he slowly sold his land off as he got older. I can work with what's left, hopefully the house doesn't need a shit-ton of repairs.

"Allie! Earth to Allie," Meko's voice finally breaks into my daydreaming.

"Yes dear," I slowly look to him, his face unhappy.

"You know this is going to be a lot of work, right?" He tells me dryly.

"Whatever, it looks like we can handle it. You know how much this means to me," I reply, walking over to him and giving him a big hug. "Plus, this will give you more time to write your next bestseller."

"Hopefully the country air will clear my head," Meko sighs as we walk to the house. "First order of business is to grade this driveway. It's so overgrown."

"The lady I talked to said the keys would be in the planter by the front door," I tell him as we walk up the steps of the old farm house.

So far, the outside doesn't look horrible. There's a lot of dirt to be cleaned off, as well as chipped paint that will need to be sanded and then repainted. Projects to keep me out of Meko's hair while he writes. As we enter the house, the doorway opens right into a nice size living room. Off to the left, I can see the dining room that leads into what I can only guess is the kitchen. As I turn following Meko into the living room, I see something out of the corner of my eye. I grab Meko's arm as I gasp.

"Allie, what is it?" He asks as he looks at me.

"There… there was a lady in the hallway," I manage to get out as I look back to see nothing.

"Is this old house already playing tricks on you, honey?" Meko laughs it off as he keeps moving through the place.

I try to shake it off, but the feeling that the woman is still there haunts me.

I don't fucking believe in ghosts. It had to be a trick of the eye.

The rest of the house is about the same; sturdy, but needs some good TLC. Poor Gramps tried his best to keep up with it until the end. I did my best to try and talk him into moving to the city with us, but he wouldn't budge. Our move here is for a fresh start. Forgiveness isn't something that comes easily to me, but when I found out I was pregnant. I decided to give our marriage another chance.

Meko promised the lies and cheating would stop; all that was important was fixing us. He wanted to be with me and a father to his child.

Gramp's death took its toll on me, Meko was my rock. He never once complained when I would burst into tears. My emotions seem to be so out of whack since getting pregnant. I'm only four months along now, five more to get through. Hopefully I'll go back to being myself soon.

"Allie, do you want to sleep here tonight or in town?" Meko asks, breaking me from my thoughts as we stand in the guest room.

"Here is fine," I smile weakly at him. "I'll throw these in the wash and we can sleep in here tonight."

"You don't want to sleep in the main bedroom?" He asks with a confused look on his face.

"That's his bed. Once our stuff gets here tomorrow we can move it in there, but it would be weird to sleep in his bed," I tell him as I start to gather the bedding to take to the washer.

"As you wish honey," he replies as he moves out of my way. "I'll start in the kitchen. That way we can have room when we go get groceries." With that he leaves the room.

Meko is really trying, I've seen a wonderful change in him since everything happened. Still, the trust I have in him isn't what it once was. I can see how much he's trying, which brings tears to my eyes as I head to the laundry room. These feelings need to get into check, I can't keep crying over nothing.

Thankfully Gramps still had plenty of laundry soaps and cleaning supplies, so while the wash is going I get to work on the bathroom. A shower would be wonderful right now, but not until it's cleaned. I open the window to get some airflow into the bathroom before getting started. The state of the bathroom is pretty clean, as with everything else, there's just a fine layer of dust on it. Gramps must have had someone coming over and cleaning, so it was pretty quick to clean in here. The toilet was first, followed by the sink, now I'm on to the tub.

Meko appears in the doorway, "Allie, once you're done let's go into town, grab lunch and get some stuff to stock the kitchen."

"Sounds great. I'm pretty much finished up in here, just need to rinse the tub and I'm done," I stand now and grab my bucket from behind me to rinse the tub.

As I turn back, there's the same woman from the hallway laying in the tub, I let out a yelp as she looks up at me. She's so pale, but what I notice most of all is the sadness in her eyes. Bandit runs in to check on me, I didn't know he was in the house. I turn back to the tub, she's vanished. I must just be exhausted from the trip, just my brain playing tricks on me. Once I have a good night's sleep, my prego brain should hopefully do better. Bandit barks; he must be hungry too.

"Meko," I call to him. "Have you fed Bandit yet? He looks a bit hungry too."

The mangy mutt barks again, like he's answering me.

"That's what I'm doing," I hear him yell from somewhere in the house.

Bandit takes off as soon as he hears the food drop into his bowl, making me laugh. Such a silly dog. I rinse out the tub then wash my hands. Food is sounding better and better. It's going to be fun finding out what we have close by. I know we won't be able to find as much as a big city, but this new adventure is going to be worth it.

I find Meko in the kitchen, "Food is sounding really good. I just need to put the sheets in the dryer."

I run and move the sheets over real quick, then meet Meko who's already waiting in the truck for me. He must be really hungry, because I know how much he loves to shop. The drive into town is a little over twenty minutes. That's not so horrible, except maybe when I go into labor.

Chapter Two

CUTE SMALL TOWN

We find a cute little cafe to eat at called, Kim's Place. Nothing fancy about it. On the right there are booths and to the left is a counter with stools where you can sit at. My eyes can't believe how packed this place is. There was only one booth open when we stepped in the joint. Thankfully the table is clean. We find the menus on the table in between the napkins and salt & pepper shakers.

A young woman no more than nineteen appears at our table with a tablet in hand, greeting us with a huge smile on her face. "How are y'all doin'?" she asks in a super sweet southern accent; the smile never leaving her face.

"Exhausted and hungry," I give her a small smirk.

"Well we can help you with the hungry part. The tired part, not so much but we do have a good B&B just down the road. They always have room for travelers. So for now, can I start you off with a drink?"

"I'll have water." looking to Meko who hasn't said a word.

"Oh is it my turn to finally talk?" Meko teases. "I'll have a Dr. Pepper please."

"Oh yeah I'm Katie. I'll be helping you today, so I'll be back in two shakes!" she squeals and rushes off.

"Isn't she a breath of fresh air?" I ask Meko before looking to the menu to see what I might like.

"Here you go, dolls," Katie is already back with our drinks. "Our special today, I forgot to tell you, is chicken fried chicken, mashed potatoes with brown gravy, and a side of green beans."

"Wow that sounds really good," Meko sounds excited by the special.

"I think that sounds delicious. I'll take it," I smile patting my stomach. "But no gravy please. Ooo and extra mashed potatoes please."

"Ditto for me please," Meko grins at me, "Now don't eat too much Allie, we have a shit-ton of cleaning to get done at the farm."

"Oh what farm are you guys staying at?" Katie inquires as she jots down our order.

"We just moved into the old Wilson place," I inform her. She kind of gives me a weird look, but says nothing.

It eats at me that she doesn't say anything, but I have a problem with dwelling on things. Maybe I shouldn't have told her where we are staying yet. Let people wonder until we are more familiar faces in town. Meko says nothing to me while we wait for our food. There is obviously something very interesting on his stupid-ass phone. This shit is the reason we left the city, more time for the two of us. I know our love is still there, and it can only grow now that we have a little one coming.

"Can you please put your phone up?" I ask him, a bit annoyed with his lack of attention.

"Sorry, I just got a crap load of emails that needed to

be answered. All book stuff." he doesn't even look up from what he's doing.

"Well don't get used to this," I want to be snarky, but I'm not sure he even heard me.

Katie comes almost skipping over with our plates, "Here's your food. Be careful, it's hot." her cheeriness is almost infectious. She wants to make me grin just for being near her.

If I was a bit younger, I could see myself hanging out with her. Not that I'm old, twenty-four probably isn't too much older then her. Marriage is just making me feel old. Meko still hasn't taken his face out of his fucking phone; he's really starting to piss me off.

"I hope she's worth it!" I spit at him as I start cutting my chicken.

I don't look at him again. He tries to reply, but I just ignore his words. Two can play his petty games. I just enjoy my food and think of all the work to be done in our new home. Who knows, I may even write my own book. Of course if I do, Meko mustn't know about it until it's done. He'd probably rip it apart. I've seen how hard he is on his own work. Today, I'll stick with shopping for food and cleaning up the house. A nap also sounds great right about now.

"When are you going to be done being pissy at me Allie?" Meko is finishing up his food now.

"I haven't decided yet. I get you have things you need to do for work, but we just fucking got here. You can't even give me a moment of your time?" I can feel the tears welling up in my eyes. "Like we are supposed to be working on giving us a fresh start, yet it doesn't feel like much has changed other than the fact the whore isn't here."

Yup, I don't regret saying it. Meko looks hurt at my words, but thankfully Katie appears at just the right time.

"So you two crazy kids leave any room for desert?" she inquires.

"No, I'm so full I couldn't eat another bite but thank you. Just our check please," I tell her nicely, I'm sure she could see the tears I was fighting back. Katie hands the bill to Meko from her apron. I grab my purse and bolt from my seat as soon as she walks the other way. Things don't feel any different. I know it's supposed to take time but hell, if I wanted to be second again we could have just stayed in the city. A walk will be nice to clear my head. This baby is wreaking havoc with my emotions.

The walk is nice; the country air is so refreshing. I'm not sure where I'm walking, but I just had to get away. Looking at all the small shops, I see a hardware store at the end of the block. Perfect. I make my way in to see what all they have, since I'll need supplies to fix up the house. My phone starts ringing right as I enter the quaint place. I silence my phone, not ready to talk to the asshat. Just needing to breathe. This store is like I stepped back into the 1950's. It's like déjà vu. Gramps brought me in here as a teen. I really should have come back to visit him more often.

Gramps tended to his farm, pretty much keeping to himself. My grandma passed when my father was very young, so I never got to know her. Gramps never did remarry, he always made excuses as to why he hadn't.

"Can I help you Ma'am?" a voice from behind me asks, making me jump a little.

I turn around quickly to find a teenaged boy; he can't be more than sixteen. Tall, skinny frame, a face full of acne, braces for days but the sweetest smile. I can't see his eyes because of his shaggy brown hair.

"You shouldn't sneak up on people! I could have peed myself! Or hit you!" I laugh. "I'm just kinda looking around."

"Well I'm Alex, and if you need help just give me a holler," he gives me a huge smile and walks away.

As he leaves, Meko finds me. I give him an eye roll.

"Allie, can you please just talk to me?" Meko pleads as I try to walk away from him.

"What, now that your face is finally out of your phone you want to talk to me?" My mood towards him has only become more foul.

"Baby, please stop. You know I have work stuff to do. It doesn't stop. Not even with this move," His voice sounds sincere, but I've believed him before.

"Bullshit!" I spout at him as I turn to finally face him, trying to hold my ground, "They knew you needed a couple days off to get moved and settled in. So fuck off if you can't even give me that."

I stomp off to find Alex. I'm going to buy some paint, brushes and sandpaper. I need a project to keep me busy once we are all moved in. Alex is more than happy to help, and he even carries it all the way to our truck. Meko is in there pouting, but I'm done being mad and put it on the back-burner, maybe. Alex knows to put everything in the bed of the truck for me as I get back in the passenger seat.

"Did you buy the whole store?" Meko tries to lighten the mood.

"Shut it. I'm not done being mad at you yet," I tell him, closing the truck door. "Let's just get some groceries and get back to the house. I'm over this." Just hearing his voice makes my blood boil, even though I'm trying my best to let it go.

Chapter Three

HORRIBLE BREAKFAST

Meko and I don't talk the rest of the night. Mainly it's just me not wanting to talk to him. Dinner is ramen noodles; quick and easy for the first night. Then I find some things to do to avoid him until bedtime. Slipping into clean sheets after a long day of cleaning is so satisfying. My hair is still wet from my shower.

Meko tries to hop into bed. I tell him, "If you're thinking of getting your ass in this bed before you've taken a shower you better think again asshole," I'm pointing my finger for him to head back out of the room. He sulks out of the room knowing he hasn't taken one yet. "I left you a towel on the cabinet."

I must've fallen asleep before Meko came to bed. With a yawn I get up to the smell of coffee brewing downstairs. Digging around to find my phone under my pillow, I unplug it to see the time, then head out to find my husband. He's cooking away in the kitchen, dancing to whatever music is in his headphones. His short blonde hair is a mess, he must not have combed it yet. I can't help but laugh.

"What the hell?" I say loud enough for him to hear me.

Meko jumps, taking his headphones off as he turns around to look at me. I'm snort-laughing now from the surprised look on his face.

"What, did you not think I'd be up? Or have you seen her?" I question him. Maybe I'm not crazy and there's someone in this house with us.

"Her? Her who? You're the only woman I've seen in this house since we got here," He gives me this look like I'm being stupid.

"You can stop looking at me that way. I know what I saw." I grumble as I sit at the kitchen table. "Now feed me whatever you're making, it actually smells good."

"The movers should be here in about an hour or so. They called to let me know where they were," he smiles as he already had a plate made up for each of us. "You were snoring so loud, I'm surprised you didn't wake yourself."

"Yeah, you're going back down the path of me not talking to you again," I say, scowling at him as I look at my plate filled with biscuits and sausage gravy. "One, I need something to eat this with please. And two, I haven't been sleeping well. I'm so sorry."

Meko starts rummaging around in a drawer, then quickly comes back to the table with forks for both of us. He hands me one as he sits across from me.

"Anyways, we will need to be ready to let the movers know what we want to keep and if we want anything taken out," Meko tells me as he digs into his biscuits.

"I really feel the only things we need moved out are Gramp's bed, and the living room furniture," I yawn, cutting my food with my fork. "After this I'm going to take a walk around the property. I just want to see all the work we have outside, too."

"I can go with you, if you'd like," His eyes light up at the idea.

"No, I may not be back before the movers come and someone needs to be here," I can see my words rip a little hole into his heart.

I struggle to get my breakfast down. Meko is not allowed to make the food again! Not having the heart to tell him, I eat every bite, acting like it's delicious. He gets done eating before me and is already getting dressed for the day when I make it back to the room.

"Are you going to sulk all day?" I ask him as he passes me without a word.

He just grunts as he walks out of the room. Laughing right now would only piss him off more, so I don't.

Today feels like a day for comfy clothes. Lots of unpacking to be done. So it's a sweats and t-shirt for me. I'm so ready to be moved in; everything is so hard to find. My socks were hiding in a pair of my pants in the bag. Once I get them on, next are my shoes. Bandit is patiently waiting for me at the back door.

"You are such a silly dog. You could have gone out the doggie door you goof," I give him a scratch behind his left ear, then proceed to open the door for us both.

Chapter Four

BEAUTIFUL LAKE

Ten acres seems a lot bigger when you are walking it. Bandit is zooming around me, loving having a yard. Every step I take, I watch for the damn dog as he keeps running in front of me.

"I will put you on a leash if you don't behave, young man!" I scold him, but he pays no mind to me as he is so carefree.

I can't wait for my little one to be running alongside this crazy dog in this cool morning air without a care in the world. Life can only get better from here. My eyes catch a glimmer coming from the left of me. Looking over, I find a pond with a small dock. This is something nice to find, as I start walking to see just how big it is. Suddenly, there's a splash. I run to the dock to find Bandit swimming in it. That silly dog has no fear, but now he will need a bath for sure.

"What is wrong with you, boy?" I laugh as he swims around in the lake. "At least you are really enjoy…" my words get caught in my throat, only to be replaced with a scream.

A woman's body is floating face down in the pond, dark brown hair with a flowing white dress. My hand immediately comes up to my mouth, and in a blink of an eye...she's gone! Bandit's out of the water, and I hear the clacking of his paws on the deck behind me.

What is it about this place that's making me crazy? Could this be my pregnant brain getting to me? Once I find a doctor here, I'll have to ask them what could cause me to see things. Then again, I have been tossing and turning a lot lately.

"Let's go Bandit," I say, looking down at my soaking wet dog. "You need a bath, you turd-head."

When we make it back to the farmhouse, the movers have shown up. They are already working hard to get our stuff moved into Gramp's place. Meko's eyes connect with mine as I look to the house. His face is a mix of fear and relief as he rushes over to me.

"Where the hell have you been?" He asks, anger in his tone.

"I told you I was going for a walk. Not really anything to get your panties in a wad about." Annoyed by his attitude as I try to move past him to go into the house.

He grabs my arm, turning me to look at him. "You've been gone for two hours!" His hazel eyes burning into mine.

"Well, we knew phones don't work out here," I shrug, trying to loosen his tightening grip. "Now get your fucking hand off my arm! I've thought of a couple other things they can take. If you don't watch it, it'll be your shit!" Giving him a smug smile as he finally releases my arm.

Bandit is right behind me as we enter the house. The poor movers look worn-out already, so I go get them both a bottle of water from the fridge to help cool them down.

"Hey guys. I know I said I only wanted the bed taken

out of the main bedroom, but is there any way these sofas could go also?" They both nod their heads yes. "Also, we brought our dining room table plus washer and dryer. So the old ones need to go out as well." I don't give them time to answer, just start pointing out what needs to leave.

I might have gone a bit overboard, but most of Gramp's stuff was outdated or plum falling apart. That man didn't like to get rid of anything. Meko is sulking in the kitchen as I have them take the table and chairs.

"Wow, you change your mind fast don't you?" He scoffs.

"I can easily point at you and they'll take you with them, asshole." I'm not over him hurting my arm over me going on a walk. "Now go unhook the washer and dryer; they will be taking those too."

"Fine. Our bed is in your grandpa's room if you want to make it up," he tells me as he stomps off to the washroom.

"That's fine. And when you're done dear, Bandit needs a bath. He found the lake before I did and took a dip before I could stop him," I can feel my smirk as I walk towards the bedroom.

Chapter Five

DO YOU BELIEVE IN GHOSTS?

*J*t's going to be so nice to sleep in my own bed again tonight. Hopefully I'll get a good night's sleep in it. It doesn't come as easy as I'd like, tossing and turning till I finally drift off.

All of a sudden I'm awake, frozen in place as the woman in the white dress walks across the room. She is so close to me I can almost touch her, and she looks as if she's crying. The fear is temporarily immobilizing my body. When I finally get the nerve to reach out and touch her, she disappears from right in front of me. Bandit barks behind me, making me jump out of my tennis shoes.

"Aren't you supposed to be taking a bath?" Bandit barks at my words. "Meko, could you hurry? Bandit is trying to get on the bed with his wet butt."

I hear some grumbling coming from the other room, then yelling. "Well, I'm trying to get this shit unhooked. What the fuck do you want me to do first? I can't do them at the same time!"

"Well hurry up! I don't want his wet ass on my bed,

especially once the new sheets are on." I laugh, knowing how much fun Meko's having.

Thankfully, I thought ahead and packed clean sheets and bedding with us in the car. Once I wrestle Bandit out of the room, I close the door quickly so he can't come back in. The bed was easy to make once I didn't have to fight that silly dog. My stomach starts rumbling. A trip into town to the cafe for food is in order. I'm too tired to cook, and I've only really made this bed. Looking around, I'm exhausted just thinking about what all needs to be done.

Food! Food comes first.

Finally leaving the room, I yell out "Meko! I'm going to grab food for everyone from the cafe. I'll be back shortly."

"Did you at least change into some real clothes?" he yells back at me.

"These are real clothes," I mutter as I grab the truck keys and my purse, then head off before he can say another word.

The music blares as the truck zooms down the old dirt road. I love rocking out, it makes me feel free. The drive into town feels a lot faster when I drive. Pulling into town, it seems to be a lot busier. Maybe I should have changed and put on a bit of makeup.

I'm a trainwreck. Too late, I'm already here and beyond starving. Trainwreck city here I come!

I try to find a parking spot close by, but it's impossible. Katie greets me as I walk in, taking a seat at the counter.

"I'll be right with you hun!" Katie whizzes by me.

I have settled on burgers and fries before stepping foot inside. Who doesn't like a good burger? Katie doesn't take too long to get back to me. It's like her smile never leaves her face.

"It's nice seeing you again so soon! What'll you have?" Katie asks as she bites on her pen.

"Four cheeseburgers and fries. Can you put the veggies on the side? I'm not sure what the movers like." I ask.

"Oh, of course. So that answers my next question. I'll write 'to-go' on the ticket." She gives me a wink. "We'll have it out in two jiffs."

I smile at her words. I'll just be the homeless looking lady waiting on a shit-ton of food. Thankfully my belly hasn't started showing yet or I'd look like a real bum. I take my phone out and flip through Facebook while I wait. I post a status update about moving in, and then Katie comes back over to give me my check.

"So they said about five minutes until yours is ready. So I thought I'd get your payment. That way you could get your food and go."

"Oh, you don't like homeless people in here, do ya?" I joke.

Katie's face goes pale, "Oh hun, what happened? That jerk of a husband kick you out?"

"No I was joking," I laugh and snort at her words. "But I would so kill him first. That's my fucking house and land! My Gramps left it to me."

"Good to know. I was wondering how you knew Mr. Wilson. So the total is $34.46." She smiles and has her hand out for the card.

I hurry and dig in my purse to pull out my card, finally finding it at the bottom of my bag. Katie takes the card out of my hand before I even have it fully out of my purse.

What the hell?

Katie bebops back to me in no time with my card and receipt to sign. "So, have you seen anything weird since you been out there? At the farm, I mean."

"I'm not sure what you mean." Giving her a look as I take the paper out of her hand to sign.

"Nothing out of the ordinary? Haunting perhaps?" Katie gives me a nudge.

"Haha," lightly escapes my lips. "Why on Earth would you think my place has ghosts? Plus, I don't believe in them." Trying to shake off her words, everything I've seen since I got here tells me otherwise.

"I've heard the stories of the woman in white that haunts the lake and house. We would go out there at night and sneak onto the land to see if we could get a glimpse of her," This is the most serious Katie has ever been as she tells me her tale. "They say she calls for her child that she drowned in the lake."

"Strange," is the only word that seems to want to come out.

"But you know how people talk in a small town," Katie's name is called and she zooms off to come right back with my order, all bagged up for me to go. "Welp, if you do, let me know. I've always wanted to see a real live ghost!"

"Isn't that a contradiction? Ghosts can't be alive," I laugh as I get up. "But I will for sure tell you if anything goes bump in the night."

With that, I leave and head back to the farm. Has Gramp's place been haunted all this time and I never knew it? Wouldn't I have seen said apparition before now? My mind has so many things going through it, I was on autopilot getting back to the house.

Meko is on the porch chatting with the movers when I pull up. Once the truck's in park, I turn it off, grab the bag and get out. The movers look happy to see the food, Meko not so much. He thinks I should always look my best when leaving the house, but I could give two shits.

"I just got us all cheeseburgers. I hope that's ok. Plus fries," they nod their heads and smile.

"We don't have a lot of people go get us lunch. Thank you," the tall, skinny one says as I hand him his box.

"Well I can't let you guys go hungry. You are doing so much for us, this is just a little perk." I wink as I hand the other worker his. "You guys can come in and eat inside if you'd like."

Bandit greets me as I walk into the house. At least he's always happy to see me. After wolfing down my food, I mentally go through the list of things I'd like to get done today. My goal is to get everything out and completely comfortable for us. Meko finishes up with the movers as I work away on what was once Gramps' room.

Every little thing I take away that is Gramp's and replace with ours is bittersweet. Not everything that is his will be gone, I want to be able to feel his love still in this house as I always have. Coming to visit him was always my favorite vacation. Not sure how they kept the lake from me though.

Knock, knock.

I jump at the sound. "Are you trying to scare the shit out of me?"

"Sorry, I had to get your attention somehow. You've been ignoring me all day! Plus the music's been on full blast while you've been working away in here," Meko states.

"I'm just tired of your shit. I'm just not going to put up with it anymore. And when I think you're being a douchebag, I'll let you know. If we are going to make this work for us, and our baby, we need a hundred percent honesty," giving him my sternest face. "And honestly, right now I feel like we are just going through the motions."

"I'm fed up. I just don't know what more I can do to gain your trust back. We moved here to get a fresh start, but all you do is throw Heather in my…"

"Your whore's name is not to be said in this house, or ever again! Got it?" I storm off before any more words can be uttered.

A shower is just what I need to clear my head. Also, I'm covered in dust and grime. Showers have always had a way of making me feel better. No worries in there, just me and the hot water. I was so mad, I'd forgotten to grab any clean clothes. Thankfully, I'd left some towels in here earlier. When I'm done, I turn the water off, pulling the shower curtain back. Words have been written on the foggy mirror.

Liar Liar Liar

A scream comes from my mouth before I know what I'm doing. Meko's right there banging on the doors trying to get in, yelling my name.

"I saw a mouse. All is okay." Now I'm the liar, fuck. Meko wouldn't believe me. I hear him mutter that food's in the oven on warm for me, then I hear him walk away from the bathroom door. I wipe away the writing with the washcloth sitting on the sink, knowing he'll just say I wrote it to freak him out. Something really is going on here, or I have a brain tumor. I'm going for the latter. Katie might have got my brain working with those questions from the diner, but I think the locals like to scare us newbies shitless by telling us ghost stories. Then come on our land and fuck with us when we aren't home, just to get their rocks off.

I towel dry as quickly as I can, then wrap a new towel around me and begin making my way to our room to find something comfy to wear for bed. Our room is coming along nicely, it's so much easier to find everything in here. The smell of whatever Meko has cooked hits my nose. I hadn't noticed how hungry I was until then. Keeping busy has helped me focus on things that are within my control, which is something I really need at the moment.

With a pull of the oven door, there sits some tater tot casserole. One of my favorite things to eat. Meko is really kissing ass now! Huh? I don't remember getting tater tots at the store yesterday. He must have snuck them by me. Food really is my true love. Once it was Meko, but he easily replaced me. So I did the same.

Him sucking up and making this helps some. At least he does remember the little things.

Dinner hits the spot, Bandit barks at me pulling me out of my head. "You can go outside anytime you want. Just no more of the lake today." I say, giving him a stern look. He just wags his tail at me, like he's not getting scolded.

By the time I wander back into the bedroom, Meko is passed out, sprawled all over the bed. Just like him to hog the fucking bed. Crawling in I give him a push, which is harder than I thought, as he almost rolls out. It takes all of my willpower not to laugh at him. I hurry and lay down, acting as if I've been resting quietly, to act like I've been in bed.

"What the hell?" comes from his mouth as his feet hit the floor.

Trying to sound like I've just woke up, "What's all the fuss about?"

"Did we have an earthquake or something?" he asks as he adjusts himself in bed.

"Yeah, and I'm losing it." I roll over and try to get some sleep.

Chapter Six

BASTARD

Waking up to a pain in my chest, I sit straight up, frozen in place. The woman in white is sitting on Meko's chest, her hands wrapped around his throat. Her head spins to look at me, then her mouth starts to move. I can't make out what she's trying to say.

Her grip only seems to get tighter on his neck as his breathing sounds labored now. Her eyes have never left me. Finally, I'm able to pull myself together enough to say something.

"What are you trying to tell me?" Comes flooding from my lips.

Her lips move once more. It looks like 'cheats' or 'cheater', I'm just not sure. She proceeds to point at Meko's phone. As she does, the phone lights up and the woman in white is gone. I'm not sure what I find more strange, the ghost on my husband trying to kill him, or his phone having service. Reaching over Meko, who doesn't seem any wiser in what just happened, I pick up his phone to see why his phone would be lighting up so late at night.

Damn him.

Chapter 6 • 29

The phone is locked and this asshole has changed his passcode so I can't get in. Meko should really change his settings too. I can still see his text messages.

Kevin- Meko it's only been a couple days since you left but I'm missing you like crazy. I don't care if your wife is pregnant you need...

That's all I could see, damn technology. My mind is a jumbled mess, who's Kevin? Is it really Heather and he just changed her name in his phone? Has this ghost been trying to warn me? If so, why is she trying so hard to help me?

This bed isn't big enough to sleep in with him. Not while knowing what I've just found out. So much for my good night's sleep. I make my way into the other bedroom. I'm just thankful I didn't have the movers take everything in there with them.

Bandit follows me into the guest room, snuggling up to me in the bed.

Somehow sleep comes back to me, probably thanks to the wonderful dog cuddles. Bandit has always known how to calm me. I wake to Meko shaking me.

"Allie, what the hell are you doing in here?" He looks a bit lost. "You scared me half to death when I couldn't find you this morning."

"Well I'm in the house. So you found me," I tell him dryly. "I'm still a bit sleepy, so if you'd go away..."

Lying to him so he'll just go away, I roll over. I don't want him to see the hurt on my face. Today is going to be the day I dive into Gramps' things and just lose myself in making this place my own. I don't know what to do with the Meko thing yet.

How did the text make it through? Maybe we have a

signal now. My phone might be working too. Finally I drag myself out of bed, but still not ready to face Meko. I'm not ready for the real fighting to begin. He's been lying to me this whole time we've been trying to fix us. I guess I was really the only one trying to make it work for this baby.

It feels like I'm in a haze, going through the motions of getting dressed, not even paying attention to what I'm putting on. The only things I have are my baby and this farm. I'll be damned if Meko and his whore take either from me.

"Breakfast is getting cold!" Meko yells at me from downstairs.

No one asked him to cook, he's probably poisoning it. Trying to kill me, or make me crazy so he can get me out of the way. Just so he can get his hands on the money my parents left me, that he can't touch unless I'm mentally unfit or dead.

Fucker. Not going to happen.

"Sorry, I was going into town to get a couple things and was going to grab breakfast there," Wow. I suck at lying. "Plus, I want to look into something about this land."

I slip into my flip flops, grab a hair brush and my makeup bag and head out of the house, before he really has a chance to follow me. By the time I'm backing up in the drive, Meko is on the porch, shirtless, yelling something at me.

Fuck him.

Tears come streaming out as I make my way down the drive. Finally, I stop at the end of our driveway and just let it all out. Sometimes a good cry is all you need, and Hell knows I did before my rage sets in. I've been trying to keep my emotions in check so I don't harm the baby, but Meko's not making this easy.

Food is the first thing on my list once in town. The second thing is to find someone who can tell me more about the farm and what's happened there. There has to be some historical proof of a death on the land.

By the time I hit town, my reddened eyes have all but gone, just still a little bit puffy. Allergies can take the blame, slapping on a bit of makeup once in a parking spot before I head into the diner. No looking like night of the living dead before I go in.

Katie welcomes me.

"Do you ever get a day off?" I smile.

"Of course, you just come in on the days I'm working." She winks at me as she shows me to a seat and hands me a menu.

I thank her and then proceed to see if anything looks even remotely good, knowing eating is a must even if I don't feel hungry.

My eyes finally fall onto the blueberry pancakes. Something Gramps used to make me every time I saw him. These will be perfect to start off my day, a sugar high. I let Katie know once she makes it back to me. This place seems like it never slows down, and this town isn't that big. They only have one stop light! Maybe people just come from all over to eat here, they've gotta have regulars too. Or everyone comes here for every meal. My prego brain is just going on overload. Just eat, Allie. And find out what might be going on in your house. Meko will be dealt with in due time, this baby and myself are my only priorities.

Katie always has a smile on her face, no matter what the day brings. I used to be like her, happy and smiling all the time. Now all I seem to do is cry. I'm not sure why I thought Meko and I could ever work through his cheating. I thought I could forgive him, but can my heart truly do it?

After seeing the texts last night, my heart shattered into a million pieces.

"Penny for your thoughts?" Katie smiles as she plops my food down in front of me.

"You don't have enough time in the day for what's going on in my head!" I try to laugh and give her a weak smile.

"Well hun, I'm here if you change your mind," she gives my hand a squeeze.

"Thank you, but I see you're super busy," with that she gets back to work.

I start in on my pancakes, with the first bite it brings memories of Gramps. The tears flow, dear God why are these hormones doing this to me? These fucking tears need to stop; I'm not sure where they keep coming from. My eyes hurt from crying and rubbing them raw. I struggle, but I manage to eat all my food. The water works have stopped, thankfully. While digging out my debit card from my purse, I find my sunglasses. These glasses will help hide my bloodshot eyes.

Katie zooms in and out with my card, wishes me a goodbye, but stops for all of five seconds when she sees I've already put my sunglasses on.

"You know it's not sunny in here, right?" she questions me.

"Yeah, thanks for the weather info, but my eyes are just bugging me. The light is just really bothering them, hence the sunglasses," I say, pulling out a smile for her.

"Well I threw my phone number in there," she says, pointing to my hand, "with your tab if you need someone to talk to."

Well my homeless look must have just moved up to that of a heartbroken pregnant wife. I'm new to all this crap, but I refuse to stay this way. I shove my card and her number into my purse, not wanting to lose either one. Then I'm off to see if I can find out anything about the property.

Chapter Seven

WHO?

Finally, I find something that might help.

"Welcome to the county records. How may I help you miss?" an older gentleman in horn rimmed glasses asks as he moves to the front.

"Ye...yes," stammering, not sure why I'm all of a sudden so nervous. Rubbing my hands on my sides to get the perspiration off of them as I'm moving closer to him. "I'm looking for any information that you can give me on the Wilson property."

"Is there anything specific you were looking for that can narrow it down?" He looks over his glasses at me as I reach his desk.

"Deaths on the property," swallowing feels hard, just saying the words out loud makes it more real.

"Getting right into it, aren't you?" he chuckles.

"Well I've heard whispers in town and now it's freaking me out a bit to stay out there," I confess, but I don't tell him I'm seeing anything.

Do I want to say a ghost? He'll probably think I'm looney if I do.

"Has Katie been running her mouth again?" his grin is only getting bigger. "That kid loves to spread rumors. Some true, but mostly just hearsay."

"Odd things have been happening out there as well. I just need to know if you have any info on the place, please," I respond, being more blunt then I'd like. "Sorry, just saying this crap out loud makes me feel crazy. I didn't mean to bite."

"My dear, it's okay. New town, new people, new everything." This man is really asking for me to hit him. Like maybe I shouldn't have apologized. "But let's get down to what you've come for. I know there is something around here." He goes over to the bookshelf behind him.

His finger trails along the books, finally landing on a spine near the bottom. With a gentle tug he pulls it out, blows the dust off, and promptly brings it over. Once back to me, he flops it on the desk, flipping it open until he finds whatever it was he'd remembered.

"Here you are, my dear. This is the only recorded death known on those lands." He points to a name on the page.

Drina Wilson

"Do you know who she is?" So many possibilities are running through my head.

"Robert Wilson's wife." He says with no hesitation.

"Can you rewind and repeat what was just said?" My head just exploded from information overload. "Are you telling me the only person on record is my grandmother?"

"One in the same," his face is puzzled. "Have you never seen photographs of her? I've got a couple on file as well."

"Yes, please. Gramps never liked to talk about her. He kept all her pics hidden away, too." I never really understood why. So my head shakes yes before I realize I'm doing it.

The gentleman trots off to a file cabinet, starting to thumb through it. Butterflies fill my stomach at the thought of seeing her for the first time. Mom was too young to really remember her, so I have nothing to go on. After what feels like an eternity of waiting, he finally comes back over to me. Giddiness is overwhelming me now, at least I think that's what this feeling is. He hands me a 5x7 black and white photograph of my Gramps and a woman. Once my eyes land on Drina's face, a shiver runs through my soul.

It's the same lady who has been scaring the ever living shit out of me on my land! But why is she doing this to me?

"Sir, do you know how she died?" My eyes never leave the picture.

"She drowned in the little lake out back behind the house. Pretty Drina had started losing it right before it happened," I can see him shaking his head out of the corner of my eye.

"What do you mean by that?" I ask, finally looking up to meet his eyes.

"Robert never let her come to town by herself much, but the last couple times she did, she was spouting off looking for someone. I could never make out who or why." He shrugs at me. "But you're welcome to keep that photograph."

"I'm going to let you keep it for now. I sure would love it, but there's so much more I need to do to get settled," reluctantly I hand it back to him. "If the offer still stands once I am completely unpacked, I would gladly love it."

Giving me a smile, he takes the photo back. "Of course, my dear. It's all yours."

"Thank you so much for your time," I say smiling back at him, then seeing my own way out. Before I walk out the door, I turn back. "I promise I'll be back real soon for that."

Chapter Eight

UNDER WATER

I'm still unsure as to what to say to Meko once I pull into the driveway. I put the truck in park and sit there for a moment, trying to gather myself. Bandit starts barking and jumping at my door, waiting impatiently for me to get out.

"Alright, alright," I tell my crazy dog as I get out of the truck.

Bandit starts running circles, which means he's ready for our walk. He's never liked taking walks with Meko, even as a pup. Which gives me pure joy.

Fuck Meko. Just fuck him and his cheating heart. The tears have all but dried up now and I'm about to go into a furious rage. Thoughts of how to kill him in his sleep creep in as I watch Bandit run free on our walk.

It's so beautiful out here, my heart could really be at peace breathing this fresh country air every day. Somehow, Bandit has brought me back to the dock and lake. The one I now know my grandmother...who Gramps acted had left us, died in. Questions are really all I have after leaving the county records office. Maybe next time I'll remember to ask the clerk's name since he was so helpful. Of course Bandit jumps right into the water as soon as we get there. That dog is going to be the end of me. He seems so happy splashing around. I started daydreaming of what it will be like to have my kiddo playing in the water with this silly dog. I must have zoned out for longer than expected. All of a sudden, I feel a hand in the middle of my back, pushing me into the lake. As the world goes sideways and the water is coming straight for me, fear fills me; Not knowing what's in here with me, as I can't see the bottom of the murky water. My breath is taken away as I hit the water, the lake is much deeper than I had imagined. I swim back up to the surface of the water. Popping back out, I spit the horrid water from my mouth that I had inhaled when I fell in. As I gulp in a large breath, something pushes me back under.

My hands go up swinging, trying to find what's holding my head under the water. I'm fighting for me and my unborn child, but there's nothing to be found. Finally, I break free of whatever was holding me there. I catch a glimpse of a man walking away as I make it to the dock, my chest heaving up and down.

"What... the... hell...?" my upper body feels like it's on fire as I slowly pull myself out of the water. I roll myself completely on the dock, just laying there until I can catch my breath.

Bandit lays down next to me, I think he can feel something is not right with me. My mind can't wrap itself around what just happened. By the time I could see clearly, the person was gone. Almost like they disappeared into thin air. Could it have been Meko? If so, how'd he get away so fast? At this point I'm just glad to be alive and praying no harm has come to my baby.

I try avoiding Meko the rest of the day, but it's pretty hard when all he does is follow me around the house. Even after telling him I just want to be left alone, he's not getting my hints.

"Leave me the fuck alone!" I finally scream at him as he follows me into the living room.

Thankfully the TV and DVD player are set up because I just want to veg out and not think of ghosts or cheating husbands.

"Fine Allie," Meko huffs. "But for fucks sake you could at least tell me what I did wrong."

He stomps off to our bedroom to give me the space I've asked for.

I grab the remote and pop the TV on. Some strange show is on that reminds me of a home movie. Lifting my hand, I hit the button on the clicker but it won't change. My eyes widen as I notice everything looks just like this house, but maybe as it was twenty or thirty years ago. The TV pans to the kitchen, a woman's cooking something. As she turns into view it's Drina, smiling at someone.

"Hi honey," she greets them.

"Where's Jake?" I would recognize that voice anywhere, that's my Gramps.

Now the TV lets me see him as well, I'm not sure if I should be freaked out or not. With everything else I've seen here this is just par for the course. Gramps sure was handsome back in the day.

"He's playing in the living room while I cook lunch," Drina informs him as she turns back to the stove.

"The hell he is!" Gramps raises his voice. "How many times do I have to tell you, you have to keep a closer eye on him?"

"I didn't know cooking lunch wasn't watching him that close. I told him what I was doing. So he knew I needed him close by." She moves the pan off the stove.

Drina races room to room trying to find Jake. He's not in the house, her face is frightened. "Robert! He's not in the house!" She screams at Gramps.

"The lake!" they both yell at the same time.

Somehow on the TV Drina makes it to the back door, scurrying down the stairs towards the lake. Drina lets out a bloodcurdling scream when she reaches the dock. The camera finally catches up to show us what she sees. Jake lying face down in the lake, not moving. Right before Gramps gets there, Drina jumps in. As she reaches Jake and flips him over, she notices something is wrong; this is not her child. Why are his clothes in the lake?

"Robert, it's not him!" She's sobbing as she swims back to him on the dock.

"Let me help you out, then we'll keep looking," Gramps offers. Drina reaches for his hand, but he puts it on her head and pushes her under the water. "I'm sorry my dear, this is for the good of us all."

That's the last thing I hear before the TV goes black.

"YOU'RE NEXT!"

Flashes on the screen before going back to saying "Insert DVD". I'm not entirely sure what's just happened. Thankfully, Bandit must feel my unease as he trots into the living room.

"I'm so glad to see you boy," he turns his head to the side like he's puzzled about what I just said. "How about we get some food and find a book to read?"

Bandit barks as if he's agreeing with me. My brain decides to go see if Meko wants food. As I near the room, Meko is talking to someone. This is strange, since I didn't think we had service out here yet. I get as close to the door as I can to listen to his hushed tone.

"No, you know I can't just leave her." Comes from Meko's voice then a pause . "Honey, you know I love you. We just need to wait for her to have the baby. Since you can't have kids Allie accidentally getting pregnant works out perfect for us. I can get the kid and the money. Allie will be none the wiser by the time we have it all."

There's no way he can touch the money that was left to

me. Well, not unless... I'm dead. Slowly, I back away from the door. Meko doesn't need to know I've heard any of his plans. My third step back makes the floor creaks.

Fuck.

I can blame it on the dog as I hurry to the kitchen and try to make myself look busy. My mind is all over the place. He only wants my baby and money. No way in hell will he ever get either.

A sandwich is what's for dinner, quick and easy. Plus I've been craving grilled cheese with tomato. By the time Meko makes it into the kitchen, I'm halfway done putting together the sandwich, getting it ready to put it in the pan once it's hot enough.

"Were you just in the hall?" he asks as he comes closer, taking one of my slices of tomato.

"Does it look like it?" I reply coldly, as I hold up my food.

The pan must be hot enough now, so I put the sandwich in and begin to wipe the butter off my fingers.

"I just heard a noise while I was on the phone with my editor," Meko tells me.

So he's going to lie, but that's okay at least I'm privy to his plans now. "Did you think maybe it was Bandit? Poor thing, his food bowl is probably empty."

He goes and looks, I hear him pour some food for Bandit.

"Yeah you were right, he needs some water too." He turns the sink on to fill up his bowl. "Allie, I think there's someone outside. Flip on the light for the back porch."

I grumble but do as he asks, even though he hasn't believed me the whole time I've said these things. The next thing I know, he takes off out the back door without a word. I turn the stove off and follow him.

Could he have seen Drina finally? Or is there really

someone out there? Thankfully the moon is full tonight or I wouldn't be able to see where I'm going. Meko is yelling at someone to stop so I just follow his voice. Just when I think I've caught up, I hear a splash.

"Help!" Meko screams.

I run a bit faster to the dock to find Meko in the water. Drina is in with him, pulling him down.

"Allie plea..." he tries, but gets pulled under again.

"I'm sorry, I can't reach you!" I shout, extending my arm out towards him. He pops back up. "Maybe next time you won't plan on killing me! You can take him, Grandma."

I turn and go back to the house. Knowing now what Drina was trying to warn me about all along. She didn't want me to die like she did, at the hands of her own husband. The stories must have come from Gramps too, telling everyone she finally went over the deep end and killed herself. Since he didn't also kill my father, Gramps sent him away and told everyone Drina had finally gone over the deep end and killed him and then herself. This is why my father wasn't welcome back here, and I could only start to visit once he had finally died.

About K.A. Morse

K.A. enjoys writing in her spare time as she has a regular 9-5 job. Of course her dream is to one day write full time. She's been married for a long time and they have one son that's almost grown. Plus 3 fat cats. K.A. loves to travel and find new holes in the wall to eat. Her goal is to one day Tavel the world and see all it has to offer (with her hubby.). While writing of course. She's a big fan of Supernatural, Doctor Who and so may more fandoms.

FB Group:
https://www.facebook.com/groups/cursedreaders
www.bookbub.com/profile/k-a-morse
https://www.instagram.com/authork.a.morse/
amazon.com/author/kamorse
www.facebook.com/kamorse1/
https://www.facebook.com/purrfectlyhauntingformatting/
twitter.com/KA_Morse1

Also By K.A. Morse

RYLEE'S AWAKENING

Rylee's Reckoning

Operation Ann: Infected Crisis

Gifted Curse (Co-write with Rinna Ford)

Goddess Of Flames

Hunter (Co-write with Jenée Robinson)

Loss of Eris (coming soon)

Anthologies:

Melissa & The Lost Tomb of Akila

Always Dreaming

With This Axe

Mania's Death (Co-write with Miki Ward)

A Date With Death (Co-write with M. Lizbeth)

Claimed

BY: SAMANTHA BEA

Ghost level

This book is dedicated to Kass. Thank you for always pushing me to get my words in.
May you always be beautifully spooky and one of my very best friends.

Author's Note

This story is a medium burn new adult traditional romance (MF). This excerpt is the first 4 chapters of Claimed, the first novel in the unnamed duet.

THIS IS NOT A COMPLETE NOVEL

Chapter One

I was only a few hours old when I was abandoned at the orphanage. Or so the story goes. I don't remember, obviously. But the nuns have told the story often enough that I feel like I do. They avert their eyes when I walk past, whispering to each other about the note they found pinned to my blanket.

Death will come for her.

The nuns think I'm evil and Wikipedia says I'm touched by death, cursed for all of eternity to live a half-life stuck between the living and the dead. Drama queens, the lot of them. However, I would rather believe either of those theories than the more realistic alternative: that the feminine scrawl on the note belonged to a drug addict, or maybe someone mentally ill with no support. Because that would be the saddest thing of all. For us both to have been abandoned by those that should have loved and protected us.

The funny thing is, sometimes I really do feel like I remember that night. Which is impossible, I know. But I remember things the nuns never mentioned. I remember the feeling of fear and confusion. I remember the feeling of death's cold fingers grasping my heart. And sometimes, if I concentrate very hard — I can remember the feeling of love. But that's crazy, right?

I made the mistake of mentioning my memories to Sister Bethesda once and she turned so white, I thought she was going to faint. She made the sign of the cross and rushed off. I ended up in the Mother Superior's office and was told to stop terrorizing the Sisters. I was punished by being ordered to complete a whole Novena *while* fasting. I was finally allowed to eat once I completed the Novena. The Novena takes nine days or nine hours, but the Mother Superior always opted for days. Did you know the body can only survive eight to twenty-one days without food or water? But if you have access to water, the body can survive for up to two months without food. I was only eight years old at the time, but I learned two very valuable lessons: do not depend on anyone else for food and never confide in the nuns.

My next valuable lesson was learned at thirteen, after I began to see actual ghosts and not just "shadows," as I called them. I belatedly realized I was given latrine duty every month after the other girls caught me talking to a ghost. They didn't believe me when I tried to tell them that I was only talking to myself. They told the Sisters who then took it upon themselves to punish me without going to the Mother Superior, for which I am eternally grateful. I would much rather latrine duty over a Novena while fasting.

I stand in the courtyard of St. Agnes' Orphanage for Girls, reminiscing over the good times and the bad. Who am I kidding? The times were always bad here. I was never able to just be a child. I never lived down the curse that the nuns believed in and death followed me through every step of my life, only serving to reinforce their fears. I never had friendships, only uneasy alliances with my enemies. Everyone was afraid of me and once I learned that, I used it to my advantage. The girls stopped bullying me and the nuns stopped trying to "beat the devil" out of me. I've been waiting on this moment for all of my life.

I stand in the center of my gilded prison for the last eighteen years, my long dark hair blowing in the gentle breeze. I close my eyes and take a deep breath. *I am free.*

Chapter Two

"Adrienne!"

I am brought back to the present by Emma, my arch-nemesis-turned-postulant. Of course her evil ass would become a nun. With her blonde hair and baby blue eyes, she looked angelic. Trust me when I say she is anything but. She was always the nuns' favorite as we were growing up and the first one to run off and tattle on me if I did something that was deemed too different and therefore needed to be punished. Cue eye roll. I open my eyes and take another deep breath, resolving to be pleasant no matter how she acts.

"Yes, Emma," I question, turning to her with a smile.

"There's a car here for you," she sneers before turning on her heel and flouncing away.

"A what," I question incredulously, but she's already gone.

It's not that I didn't hear her, it's just that I don't understand why a car is here for me. Me, the girl with no friends. The girl who spent eighteen years in damn-near isolation. And a car is here for *me?*

"Well? What are you waiting for," says a grumpy voice to my right. I roll my eyes as I turn to face Mr. Grady.

"Why are you in such a rush? It's not like you're getting old while you wait," I snark back, chuckling at my own joke while he just harrumphs and crosses his arms over his faded blue cardigan. A shock of fluffy white hair falls forward into his slightly rheumy eyes and he shoves it back irritably. He swears that him dying before he could get a haircut is his personal definition of hell.

Mr. Grady has been haunting me for most of my life. He's a curmudgeonly old man who refuses to cross over. Instead, he spends his days making grumpy commentary on my life. I pretend not to like him, but I would be lost without him. He's like a grumpy old grandpa that disapproves of all your life choices, but still loves you at the end of the day. Or so I tell myself.

He's never actually told me he loves me, but I think I see it sometimes. Like when he stands up for me, even though no one can hear him. Or when he uses his limited ability to move objects in an attempt to scare away my bullies, despite it causing him to disappear for days at a time to recharge. He can never remember where he went when he comes back, but I'm just glad he always comes back. I dread the day he doesn't.

I force myself to stop procrastinating and head to the front of St. Agnes' to find out what's going on. Mr. Grady follows silently behind me as I walk through the gate of the courtyard and step onto the sidewalk. I glance up and down the street a couple times before realizing the black limousine parked directly in front of the entrance is the "car" that Emma was referring to. My eyebrows shoot up as Mr. Grady whistles under his breath.

The driver's side door opens and a man steps out, straightening his suit jacket before rounding the car and opening the back passenger door. He turns to face us, shocking me by making eye contact with both myself and Mr. Grady. No one ever acknowledges Mr. Grady because, well, he's dead.

I glance to the side and meet his eyes, noting that he doesn't look the least bit shocked. "Friend of yours," I question him in a murmur. His expression turns grim but he nods his head. That doesn't bode well.

"Miss Tanda," the man in the suit greets me as we step closer.

I stop a couple feet away, so that I'm not within arm's reach. I don't want this man to toss me into the limo before I figure out what's going on here. Glancing into the back seat through the still-open door, I can see my luggage placed neatly on the floorboard. I tighten my lips in irritation at the obvious disregard for my own wishes. I console myself with the reminder that my luggage is replaceable, but then a horrifying thought occurs to me.

"Do you have my books," I question the driver. "And just who are you, anyway," I ask before he can answer my first question.

"I apologize, Miss. My name is Hodges and your books are safely packed away in the trunk. I also apologize for placing your luggage in the back seat, but there was simply no more room in the trunk. You have quite a lot of books," he finishes, giving me the distinct impression that he's grumpy about the books despite his unerringly polite tone of voice and neutral expression.

I take a moment to commit his features to memory, in case I have to pick him out of a police lineup later. His dark hair and eyes make him look mysterious, while the scar that cuts through his right eyebrow makes him look a little dangerous. However, his perfectly fitted suit and politely modulated voice make him seem like an upper crust butler. This Hodges is quite the enigma, but I can't let myself be sucked into a puzzle. Any strange man that asks you to get in his car is automatically a threat, so I need to keep my wits about me and not get distracted like I normally do.

"You told me your name, but I'm going to need more information than that. No way in hell am I getting into a vehicle with you until I know exactly who you are," I bluff, narrowing my eyes in suspicion. But it really doesn't matter who this guy is. He's got my beloved book collection that I've spent my entire life building. He has me by the metaphorical balls, but he doesn't know that. Hodges meets my suspicious gaze calmly, showing no outside reaction to the fact that I kind of insinuated he might be a kidnapper.

"Of course, Miss. I am here on behalf of Mr. Mors, CEO of Mors Inc. and benefactor of the Mors Scholarship for Underprivileged Youth. We sent you a letter informing you that you've been selected to receive the scholarship, which includes lodging, a paid internship, and a full ride scholarship to Cornell University for the degree of your choice. Mr. Mors planned on being here, but an urgent matter arose at the last minute, so he sent me in his stead." He pauses, waiting for a response from me. However, I'm quite speechless at the moment. Lodging? A *paid* internship? A *full ride* scholarship? He looks away from me to check the time on his pocket watch and I take the opportunity to pinch myself while he's preoccupied. Just to make sure.

Hodges' mouth quirks the tiniest bit and I realize he must've seen me. And now he's laughing at me. Just great. A butler with the emotional range of a pillowcase, who has probably never laughed in his life, is laughing at me. I swear life is just one big joke and I'm the butt of it.

"I guarantee that you are not dreaming, Miss Tanda," Hodges states, proving that he did indeed see me pinch myself. But he's wrong. Good things like scholarships don't happen to the likes of Adrienne Tanda. I'm suddenly impatient to be done with this farce.

"Listen, *Hodges*. I never applied for any scholarships, much less this Mors Scholarship for Underprivileged Youth. And I definitely never received a letter stating I was awarded the scholarship. I think I would have noticed getting mail after eighteen years with no correspondence," I finish, rolling my eyes.

"Mr. Mors thought you might be skeptical, so he prepared this for you." Hodges reaches into the back seat of the limo and pulls out a glossy black folder with Mors Scholarship for Underprivileged Youth printed across the front in white script. I can already tell this place is going to be too classy for me, but I push aside my reservations and take the folder Hodges' outstretched hand. I open the folder and read the handwritten note silently.

The Mors Scholarship does not accept applications. We seek out deserving scholars among the underprivileged youth in America; scholars who may not have been able to attend college otherwise. We have awarded this scholarship to you, Adrienne Tanda, based on your individual merits. Enclosed, you will find a brochure for Cornell University, a private research university in upstate New York. Mors Inc. has worked closely with Cornell University on many research projects. In return, they have agreed to our scholarship program. You will be allowed to choose your own classes and schedule. You will also find a brochure on Mors Inc., along with several options for your paid internship. Finally, you will find a brochure on Mors Manor, where you will be lodging during the course of your studies and internship. If you accept this scholarship, you also agree to the internship and lodging described above. If you renege on the internship or lodging, you will lose your scholarship.

Please inform Hodges of your decision and he will proceed accordingly.

Signed,

Samuel Mors

Once I'm done reading, I take a moment to flip through the enclosed brochures. There is indeed a brochure for Cornell University (Cornell!), Mors Inc., and Mors Manor. I can't believe this is happening, but I know I have to take this opportunity. Cornell University is everything I've ever dreamed of and never in my wildest dreams thought I would have within my grasp. The Mors Inc. job descriptions sound unique and interesting, which is more than I can say for my barista job. Mors Manor looks like the house in X-Men and I can't decide if that's a good thing or a bad thing. I am a huge DC and Marvel nerd, after all. I come to the end of the last brochure and take a deep breath before changing my life forever.

"I accept."

Chapter Three

"Don't think it's escaped my notice that you've been as silent as a church mouse during all of this," I state, turning away from the scenery outside the limo window to face Mr. Grady in the seat across from mine. He has the good grace to look ashamed, but he meets my eyes determinedly. I wait for a moment, but he doesn't speak.

"Do you want to tell me how Hodges can see you? And why you seemed to know him," I ask, rapid-firing questions at him quicker than he can answer.

He rolls his eyes as he replies, "Did you think you were the only person who can see ghosts? Anyone with a pinky full of The Sight can—" He cuts off before he finishes, looking horrified.

"The Sight," I start to ask, but it's too late. He's already gone, poofed off to God-knows-where.

I sigh, leaning into the door as I resume watching the scenery fly by. Mors Manor and Mors Inc. are both located in Ithaca, New York, where Cornell University is. Which is very logical and highly convenient, two of my favorite words. I've never been to upstate New York, but I know it's about four hours from New Jersey. Don't ask me how I know. I think all New Jerseyans know exactly how far they are from New York at any given time. The mutual dislike between New Jerseyans and New Yorkers runs deep.

But despite my predilection to hate New York (and New Yorkers, of course), I have to admit that upstate New York is beautiful. Especially this time of year, when the trees have all changed colors for fall. Fall is my favorite time of year. I love how the world looks when it is getting ready to shed its shell and start anew. There is just something so beautiful about that.

I glance at my watch and groan. I still have three and a half hours left until we arrive at Mors Manor. I doubt Mr. Grady is going to pop back in to keep me company after his hasty departure. Pushing aside the mystery of what he meant by "The Sight," I grab the folder to look through the Cornell and Mors Inc. brochures. With all this time on my hands, maybe I can decide on my classes and internship.

Three hours later, I am even further from a decision than I was before I started. The problem is, there are just too many amazing choices! I've always wanted to be a writer, and I've even been published (in our school publication, but still). I just never dared to dream that I could attend college. My meager dreams consisted of leaving the orphanage to live in a halfway house until I could save up enough with my barista job to rent a small studio apartment. Speaking of, I better call my manager and my contact at the halfway house. I pull out my prepaid phone and check the minutes. Five minutes might last me both phone calls if I'm quick.

I call Jameson at the halfway house first, explaining that I made arrangements elsewhere and thanking him for his time and guidance over the last few months as I made the preparations to move. He wishes me luck, his voice ringing with sincerity. I quickly end the call and check my minutes. Only two minutes left, but I'll have to make it work. Luckily, I get Rita's voicemail when I call to quit. I apologize for not giving her notice and end the call before my minutes can run out and cut me off. And none too soon, as my phone now shows zero minutes. I make a mental note to refill it after I get my first paycheck.

I glance up as the scenery changes outside the window. We pull up in front of a wrought iron gate with a sickle emblem on both sides. Hodges presses his thumb to the keypad and I watch in silence through the front windshield as the gate opens to reveal a long gravel driveway with a massive manicured lawn on either side. Hodges pulls forward slowly and I get my first view of Mors Manor in person. It's absolutely massive, even bigger than in the photos. *That's what she said.* I snort to myself at my stupid joke.

Hodges pulls up in front of the steps and comes around to open my door for me, but I open it and jump out before he gets there. He glares at me without really glaring. This man really has a gift of conveying emotion without actually showing any emotion. *Maybe he'll teach me how to do that.*

"Right this way, Miss Tanda," he states, gesturing up the steps. I reach the door and do a double take. Somehow he reached the door before I did, even though I walked ahead of him. *Curiouser and curiouser.* He opens the door for me and shows me to a small sitting room off of the main foyer.

He walks to an adjoining door and knocks briefly before a deep voice commands, "Enter." I only get a brief glance into the doorway before he disappears into the dimly lit room beyond. I didn't see much, but the walls looked to be lined with books. I rub my hands together greedily. I really hope that room is open to my use.

I notice a cocktail table in the corner of the room with a pitcher of water, a container of ice, and a few glasses on top. I'm more nosy than I am thirsty, so I walk over to the table and grab a glass. I walk quietly back to the door and place the glass against the wood so I can eavesdrop. I've only ever seen this in movies, so I'm surprised when it actually works and I can hear the conversation clearly.

"Does she suspect," the deep voice asks, the timbre of his voice running a shiver down my spine. If there was ever a perfect definition for "bedroom voice", this is it.

"No sir, she has no idea. She was suspicious at first, but she thought I was there to kidnap her," Hodges replies, amusement lining his voice. That's more emotion than he's ever let show around me, so he must be quite comfortable with the mystery speaker. I'm guessing the deep voice belongs to Mr. Mors, but I'm not sure.

I'm so confused. If they aren't kidnappers, what are they worried about me finding out? What could possibly be worse than kidnapping? Murder? But why go to all the trouble with this elaborate ruse? Oh God, is this some human trafficking ring? I glance to the open sitting room doorway and the clear path to the front door. No, that doesn't make sense. If this was a human trafficking ring, they would have locked me up as soon as we got here. It must be something else. Maybe this scholarship is a cover for their shady business dealings. Is there a mafia in upstate New York? Ithaca would be a damn weird location for mob business, but what do I know? I'm just a girl from Jersey, where mobsters perform their business out in the open and pay cops to look the other way, like normal mobsters.

"In a way, I suppose you were," the voice replies. *Wait, what?*

"Sir," Hodges replies, sounding scandalized. "I am no kidnapper," he huffs.

There's a deep sigh before the other voice replies, "She deserves to know the truth. It is well overdue. Please send her in, Hodges."

"But, sir," Hodges tries to argue, but he's cut off.

"Thank you, Hodges."

"Sir, please re--"

"I *said*, 'thank you', Hodges," the deep voice interrupts Hodges again, this time with a warning threaded through his voice. The room immediately falls silent before I hear shuffling steps headed in the direction of the adjoining door.

Chapter Four

I straighten away from the study door and tuck my hands behind my back, hiding the glass I was using to listen in on their conversation. Hodgins opens the door and gestures for me to enter the study, stepping to the side as I walk past. I step into the dimly lit room, cautiously moving forward until I reach the massive desk with a figure shrouded in darkness seated behind it. I can only hope Hodgins doesn't notice the glass still gripped in my left hand. I realize I don't have to worry about him as he exits, closing the study door firmly behind him and startling me. I lose my grip on the glass and try my best not to wince as it falls to the floor behind me, making a nearly imperceptible thud as it lands. I'm lucky this room has carpeting instead of the marble tile in the foyer. Maybe the mysterious figure behind the desk won't notice the glass lying on the carpet until I'm long gone.

"I believe you dropped something, Adrienne," the mysterious figure behind the desk states in amusement. His voice dances up and down my spine, leaving tingles in its wake. If I could bottle that up and sell it, I would be as rich as he seems to be. And then what he said finally registers and I blush deeply.

"Yes, I seem to have dropped my water glass. How clumsy," I state in a rush, crouching down to grab the glass.

"Your water glass? Do you mean your eavesdropping glass," the figure states, chuckling to himself. My jaw drops. *How in the hell did he know I was eavesdropping?* He continues to laugh and for a moment, I'm still too shocked to say anything. Then I find my voice.

I groan as I reply, "I'm so embarrassed, I could die--" I cut off as the figure straightens from the desk, standing to his full six foot plus plus plus height and moving into the lighting from the lamp across the room. I audibly gasp at how gorgeous he is, but I don't have a chance to truly take in his features before he starts speaking.

"Don't say that," he states, leaning across his desk with the most deathly serious look on his face.

"Don't say what," I whisper, having lost my voice somewhere in between the stupidly tall height and the stupidly gorgeous face, leaving me just plain stupid.

"Don't ever say you want to die," he answers, staring deep into my eyes. His eyes are as dark as mine, maybe darker. But the longer I stare, the more I swear I can see a ring of fire around his pupils.

My eyes jump back and forth between his before I finally choke out, "What *are* you?"

He grins and for a split second, his gorgeous face is overlaid with the image of a skull. It disappears as he answers, "I am Death. While I use the name Samuel Mors in this time, I am known by many different names across many different cultures, religions, and times."

I just stare at him. I think I would prefer any of my suspicions to be true, than for the benefactor of my once-in-a-lifetime opportunity to be a raving lunatic. Maybe he's just making some weird joke. Reluctant to give up my newfound dreams, I decide to play along.

"If you're Death, shouldn't Hodges have picked me up in a hearse," I question, laughing at my own joke but he doesn't even crack a smile. *Oh shit. He's serious.*

"I know you don't believe me, but let me tell you the story. Eighteen years ago, there was a woman driven mad with The Sight who left her baby on the doorstep of an orphanage. She could see the future, you see. And she saw that Death would come for her baby, so she tried to hide the baby from Death. But Death sees all. Luckily, Death found the baby in time to save her from freezing to death. But being touched by Death means that your fates are forever entwined."

To be continued...

About Samantha Bea

Samantha Bea is a displaced Cajun author that has lived in Texas most of her life, for which she can thank her mother. As a life-long writer, she uses real life circumstances to spin tales of fantasy, paranormal, and contemporary romance. When she's not plotting out the many ideas in her head, she can be found on Texas trails chasing after her dog Taz or bothering her annoyingly tall brothers.

Samantha Bea's Links

Amazon author page:
https://www.amazon.com/author/samanthabea
Facebook author page:
fb.me/samanthabeawriting
Facebook group:
https://www.facebook.com/groups/Neverneath
Facebook profile:
fb.me/samantha.bea.author
Twitter:
*https://twitter.com/samantha_bea_*
Instagram:
https://www.instagram.com/samantha.bea.author/
Booksprout:
https://t.co/lwrvjtaZ91
BookBub:
https://www.bookbub.com/authors/samantha-bea

Also by Samantha Bea

Never, Never: Book 1 of the Neverneath Series
htttps://amzn.to/2KBfn3n

Don't Puck With Her, Prequel to Don't Puck With Them (TBA),
released in the Make it Count Anthology
htttps://amzn.to/39YI5nA

Unwanted Attachments

BY: STEPHANIE HASSENPLUG

Ghost Level

Thank you to Tara, Aunt Cris, and Gabe for giving me a great experience to work with.

It's not always the home that is haunted...

Chapter One

As we pulled up to the dilapidated building, you could see it had been around for years by the bygone design. There wasn't much to the large edifice, a square front entrance with two wings that shot off from the sides. If the brick had a good power wash there would have been nothing eerie about it.

I took a long swig of my water to prepare myself for what awaited us. In the back of my mind, the voices of my cousins saying, *stop being such a wimp,* came forward. I opened the car door and stepped out; I ambled over to where my friends were leaning on the hood of the car waiting for me.

It was Halloween night, and the most haunted hospital in Texas called the Hilltown Hospital was open for tours. The neglected institution had closed in the 1980s, and all the stories I've heard had led me to believe it was chock-full of activity. I leaned against the car and folded my arms across my chest. There were a few other groups waiting to go on the tour as well.

"Tara, are you sure this is a good idea?" Rachel's

nervous voice pulled me from my observations. She leaned closer to me so none of the other girls could hear and whispered, "You know, with your sensitivity and all."

I knew I shouldn't test my luck and venture into a place like this, but you only live once. *Right?* Pushing off the car hood, I gestured to my friends to follow me.

"Let's do this!" As much I knew that this could be risky, I wanted to have a good time with my girlfriends on Halloween.

We got to the front of the building and gave the guide our tickets. The other groups saw us and began walking up to do the same. The tour guide called for everyone to follow him. He led our tour group through the mundane entrance. The air was frigid, a stark contrast to the humid warmth outside, causing goosebumps to form along my arms and I shuddered. A feeling of dread filled me and my stomach lurched. Swallowing down the bile that rose into my throat quickly, I second guessed my decision.

Ever since I was a child, I've always had a sensitivity to the paranormal. It didn't help that my mom's family had an unhealthy obsession with ghosts; I'm sure a few were sensitive like me. We'd spend get-togethers retelling ghost stories we had heard all our lives. They never got old for us. Once we were good and jumpy, my brother, older cousins, and I would spend the rest of the nights playing spot-light and scaring each other.

As the guide gave us the history of the building, my eyes scanned the dimly lit hallway. Our tour group was led down the main hallway. He walked backwards most of the time, talking about the rooms we passed. We got to the intersection where the two wings met this corridor, and he took us left. As we wandered in and out of the rooms, everyone seemed to let their guard down a bit. My girlfriends and I began to joke around quietly and laugh at ourselves for being scared earlier.

The man led us to a room filled with toys. The space had a dank smell, and the items strewn around were moldy and rusted. We weren't able to walk too far into the room, but my gut told me we shouldn't be in there. He let us know that the area in the hospital we were in was once the maternity ward as well as where pediatrics used to be. As he began to elaborate on the ward, I tuned him out and took in the surrounding room. The hair on my arms stood on end as my heart quickened. Quietly, I reached for the closest friend; I pulled her with me as I slowly backed out of the room, thankfully we were at the back of the group. Taking my cue, our other friends discreetly followed us. As we made it out of the threshold, I let go of the arm I had grabbed.

Rachel's wide eyes stared at me. "What's wrong?"

I tried to shake the panicky feeling away. "That room didn't feel right at all."

In the years Rachel had known me, she knew I wouldn't act this way for nothing and that they all needed to abide by this warning. The rest of the tour group trickled out of the room. I got a few weird looks, but most just followed along with no notice.

As the crowd moved on, we heard a small voice come from the room we had just exited. Everyone stopped in our tracks and looked back toward the room. The guide came rushing through the people. He looked way too excited to hear a random scary child's voice.

"Did y'all hear that? In the time I have worked here, I've only heard stories of the toys talking. This is awesome!" His eyes fell on me suspiciously. He must have seen us leave the room. "Did you feel something in that room? Are you sensitive by any chance? That would be awesome if you were."

"Uhhh..." Fully aware that I was, but he and the strangers with us didn't need to know.

Rachel came to my rescue, "Let's keep moving, no telling what else we'll see."

The guide's eyes lit up with the possibility of more experiences and ushered the group to follow him.

Beth's arm brushed mine as we walked. I could tell she wanted to ask something. She finally built the courage. "Tara, are you, you know, sensitive?" She didn't give me a chance to reply to her initial question and kept talking. "If so, why the hell did we come on this? It doesn't seem safe at all for you."

I nodded my head yes. "I've heard the stories and have always been curious about this place. So, I knew coming into this that something could happen, but as long as I keep my guard up, I'll be fine." My answer didn't look to put her at ease, but she nodded anyway.

"Holy hell!" Rachel placed her hand over her heart to make it more dramatic. "I almost pissed myself after we heard that devil doll." My friends and I snickered. My best friend had a way of lifting the mood, even in a serious situation.

The tour group was led to a nurse's station that was situated in the middle of the hallway. The guide started to explain the background of this area and the stories that went along with it. The large desk was full of thick spiderwebs. Thoughts of what was living in those crevices invaded my mind, and they made my skin crawl more than the idea of ghosts wandering around. While my brain was off thinking about creepy spiders, a faint squeak behind me caught my attention. Against my better judgement, I glanced back to see what it was. There was nothing there.

My mind must have been messing with me. *Right?* Maybe a mouse or something got spooked and ran across the floor before I looked.

I turned to listen to the guide. He was saying many people, as well as himself, have experienced hearing the sounds of people walking around. The man paused so we could try to experience it for ourselves. As we stood there quietly listening, you could hear faint sounds of people shuffling around and ghostly conversations going on around us. A sound from the nurses' station caught my attention. I leaned over the counter, moving my ear closer to a small, rusted speaker.

A muffled voice came through. "Help me, Tara."

I pushed from the counter quickly. The sound of my name coming through the speaker was unnerving.

When I looked around to see if anyone else had just heard what I did, Rachel's jaw was hanging. "What the F?"

The tour guide was beaming once again. "This is great! You're definitely sensitive, and the spirits are reaching out to you."

This man was crazy. No one in their right mind would be excited about a ghost calling their damn name. Absolutely no one. My thought on this was validated while I peered around at the rest of the group. They all had looks of terror as they stared back at me.

The guide moved on with excitement as we followed. A few people whispered and looked back at me. There were whispers and looks my way, but I avoided them the best I could.

We were led to an opening. It looked like a door used to hang there, but it had fallen off at some point. There was a foreboding set of stairs that looked to lead to the basement. The idea of going down into the unknown void made my heart pound. We reluctantly descended the stairs but didn't go very far into the pitch black area. Phone lights illuminated the dark. I reached into my pocket for my phone and I turned my light on as well.

"Tara, is that your name?" The guide was speaking to me, *great*. That damn ghost had to give him my name.

"Uh, yup, that's me." I did not want this attention. I shined my light toward where the guide's voice came from.

He was grinning at me. "I was thinking, you may be a great trigger object down here. Maybe the ghosts want to be friends with you. Why don't you say something to them?"

I put my arms through Rachel's and Abbey's since they were the closest. "No, thank you, I have enough friends. I appreciate it though. And, I prefer to only speak to the living." The tour group laughed uncomfortably. I don't know if it was to make me feel better, or it was because they felt bad for my actual friends.

He didn't seem too happy that I didn't want to take part, but shrugged it off and began telling us about the basement. Like many other places, the morgue was down here. He informed us that dark masses were often seen darting out from the halls. We were not allowed to explore the area due to the type of activity down here, and it was only left to professionals to investigate. When he was done, he asked the group to follow him back up the stairs. Everyone moved quickly, we all wanted out of this area. Maybe the uncomfortable energy was palpable enough for non-sensitives to feel it as well. I was almost done climbing the stairs, when something flew past my face and hit the door frame in front of me. Moisture splashed the side of my face. I shined my phone light toward the doorway and then down on the steps in front of me. A water bottle was laying there leaking water on the cement.

Again, the ever-excited guide came running through the group toward me. "What happened?"

I pointed at the ground. "Something flew out in front of me and hit the doorframe. When I looked down, this bottle was lying there."

His jaw dropped, and he looked at me, horrified. "Apologize to the ghosts now. DO IT! You have upset them by saying you didn't want to be friends. I knew I should have skipped the basement."

Tears formed in the corner of my eyes, and I pleaded to the spirits. "I'm so sorry, I'll be your friend." My pleading turned into sobs. "I'm sorry." My girlfriends grasped my hands, giving them a squeeze to reassure me they were there. Not that anyone could help me. As much as I hated it, I knew that I was triggering all this by just being here.

After I had calmed down, I wiped the tears from my eyes. When I looked around, the entire tour group was watching me with a mix of fear and pity on their faces. The guide called for everyone to follow him to the next location, taking their attention from me. We hung back for a second before following.

Rachel studied me closely. "Do you want to keep going? We can leave anytime you want, just say the word."

I shook my head, "No, no. I'll finish the tour. I have apologized to the ghosts, maybe they'll leave me alone, hopefully."

My friends didn't look so sure, but we moved along with the tour nonetheless. Again, we wandered out of rooms, getting the stories along the way. The air felt lighter in this wing of the hospital. This made me feel so much more relieved.

One of the last areas at the end of this corridor was a chapel. This room was larger, so we could move around it more comfortably. The guide explained the history, and I gazed around. Much like the rest of the hospital, this room smelled like mold and decay. The pews were all still in one piece, but you could tell that time had not been good to them. For some reason, I was drawn to the altar. I stepped up to the large wood slab; I slid my fingers along the dusty top. As I wiped the dust from the tips of my finger, I felt something run down my left cheek. Quickly swatting around me, it must have been a spiderweb. This place was full of webs.

While looking up where the crucifix used to hang, I felt an icy breath on my neck. The sensation caused me to jump. Quickly, I looked around to make sure no one was around me or noticed what had just happened. There was no one, and the rest of the group was looking around the room while the tour guide talked. No one seemed to notice, thank goodness. I briskly joined my friends to listen to the history of the room.

The guide was informing us about the nuns that founded the hospital. He then went on to say that the people that had experiences in this room were typically ones with tattoos. These incidents for tattooed people were more violent, like scratches and shoves. No one else really had any bad things happen to them.

I thanked the heavens that I hadn't gotten any tattoos yet. Just when I was about to pat myself on the back for being tattooless, my cheek began to sting. Reaching up, I ran the tips of my fingers over my left cheek. I hissed from the sting under my touch.

Rachel noticed what I was doing and grabbed my hand. "What happened?" She looked at my face where I had just touched.

"I have no idea, I was just standing here, and I felt a sting on my face."

She moved around me, checking for anything that could have done this. "There is nothing here, Tara."

I shivered, "I don't know then, Rach."

Beth and Abbey caught hold of my arms and pulled me out of the room; Rachel and I didn't object.

As soon as we exited the chapel, Abbey looked at me and then at our friends. "We are done, it's time to get out of this godforsaken place. I can't stand here and watch Tara be attacked by anything else."

The tour guide came out of the chapel and once he saw us he took a few steps toward us. He had a look of disappointment on his face. "I'm sorry, I got overly excited about the experiences we were having because of you. I think I've only helped to paint a target on your back. If you guys want to leave, by all means."

We were leaving no matter what he said, but it was nice of him to apologize. "I appreciate the apology, thank you." I looked around at my friends. "We are going to leave. This is all too much for me and my friends."

After he apologized and thanked us for coming, my friends and I all hurried toward the exit. We made it to the split that took us to the front entrance and to the other wing, when something made me turn back down the long hallway we were just in. At the end of the dark corridor by the chapel, an even darker figure stood watching us. I squinted to try to make out the mass. It almost looked like a...nun?

My body froze in terror. Fighting through the shock, I yelled to my friends, "RUN...NOW!"

The girls didn't question, and we took off in a full sprint. The feeling of someone chasing us followed me all the way out of the building. We didn't stop until we were out of that nightmare hospital. Everyone was breathing heavily and Beth skidded the car out of the parking lot.

The half hour drive was quiet, none of us talked about the experiences that occurred. I think everyone was trying to erase the events from their minds. The apparition at the end of the hall just kept flashing into my mind. I don't think I'll be able to erase the stuff that happened tonight from my brain, no matter how hard I try.

Chapter Two

We finally pulled up to Abbey's house. After saying bye, I got into Rachel's car so she could take me home. I usually drove, but my car was currently sitting in my driveway airing out. One of my dogs had spooked a skunk that was hiding under my car and it sprayed. Oh, the wonderful things about living in the country.

Rachel and I were both quiet as she drove, but after a few minutes she couldn't take it anymore. "Tara, why did you yell for us to run?"

I swallowed the lump in my throat and told her the truth. "I looked back when we got to the split in the hallways and saw a dark figure at the end of the corridor where the chapel was. My gut told me to get myself and y'all out of there. As we ran, I could feel whatever it was following us."

She cursed under her breath. "I knew we shouldn't have done this damn tour, but nooooooooo we had to go."

I chuckled at my best friend. "Well, we have an experience that is our own now."

Rachel scowled at me. "How can you joke about this? You have a damn scratch on your face from some unknown force! The doll, I can handle that, but this? No."

I totally understood where she was coming from.

We pulled through the gate at the bottom of my property. The dirt road that led up to the house made the ride bumpy. Once we were over the cattle guard, I noticed the only light on was the one above the side door. My family must have been out or asleep.

Rachel parked, and I said bye before getting out. My best friend waved before she backed out; I waved back at her. As I walked toward the porch, I realized that none of my dogs came up to me. They had come over to sniff Rachel's car, but none would come toward me. Actually, they backed away, one may have even growled. That was odd.

I huffed and walked up the steps to the porch toward the door. As usual, the door was unlocked. That was the nice thing about living in the middle of nowhere in a small town. If anyone came when we weren't home, it was just family or close friends that were trusted. The dogs would run off anyone that didn't belong here.

I closed the door quietly behind me. Bear, one of the inside dogs, was running across the living room toward me barking. He was mine and was always happy to see me. Before he got to me, he stopped and skidded on the linoleum. He sniffed the surrounding air. Bear cautiously took a step toward me.

"Hey buddy, it's just me. What is going on?" He let me pet his head for a few seconds but took off toward my room. I was left confused.

As I walked down the hallway toward my mom and step dad's bedroom I could tell the light was off and I could hear the fan going. They were asleep. That meant my younger step brother was sleeping as well. I'll tell them about tonight when we all wake up tomorrow.

I grabbed my pajamas from my room and quietly padded down the hallway toward the restroom to shower before bed. I needed to get the yuckiness of the night off my body. Maybe my dogs smelled the old building on me, I wouldn't want to greet me either.

Once I was clean and in my room, I closed the door and walked to my bed to lie down. Bear was already sprawled across my queen-size bed sleeping. I pushed the big dog over and tucked myself in next to him. He lifted his head and then went back to sleep. I must smell better now. I picked up my phone and texted my boyfriend to tell him about the night. He was concerned, but happy I made it home safely. After saying goodnight, I plugged my phone in and curled up to go to sleep.

I was awoken in the middle of the night by the weight of Bear standing over me. He was growling at the door with the fur on his back raised.

"What's wrong Bear?" I tried to push him away so I could go check the door, but he wouldn't move. "I need to go check buddy." He still didn't budge.

After a couple more minutes, he stepped over me and laid down, but kept his head on my stomach facing the door. Again, I tried to get up, but he softly growled at me to not move. Bear growled no matter his feelings, it was his thing.

"Okay, okay. Let's go back to sleep then." He seemed happy with that, and we fell asleep once again.

When morning came, Bear was already out of my room. Mom must have taken him to let him out when she got up. I walked out of my room to the restroom to freshen up. After I finished, I found mom, Gabe, my stepdad, and my little brother, Austin, in the living room. My older brother, Derek, was in the military, and he lived in Las Vegas right now.

"Morning, Tara." Mom smiled at me.

"Good morning." I dropped myself on the couch with my stepdad. "Gabe, can you hand me that blanket?"

"Yeah, sure." My step dad grabbed it and tossed the fuzzy warmth toward me. "Oh, how was the ghost tour last night?"

Everyone looked at me, "Well, it was eventful actually."

Austin perked up from his drowsy state, "For real? What happened?"

I chuckled at him. "Yeah, we heard people talking, a toy talk, I felt something breath on my neck...then something scratched my face…"

Mom jumped up, her nursing instinct kicked in. "WHAT! Let me see your face. That place is old, do you need a tetanus shot?"

I pushed her hands away. "Mom, it was just a tiny scratch, nothing big." She was reluctant but sat back down.

"That isn't it though…" I wrung my hands together before telling them the next part.

Gabe looked shook up, he was a worry-wart. "Are you kidding me, Tara? More?"

"So much more. Well, a ghost said my name, and I got a water bottle thrown at me." Everyone looked stunned for a second.

Once my mom processed what I said, she was the first to break the silence. "WHAT! Did you leave after all that?" She shook her head at me. "I'm upset you went, Tara. I knew this was a bad idea."

"I know, I know. We left the tour early; Rachel and the girls were done." I wasn't sure if they needed to know about the apparition I had seen at the end, I'll keep that one to myself.

"But when I got home, the dogs were acting weird toward me; Bear, too. None of them would come near me. Bear was okay with me once I showered and came to bed though."

Austin snorted, "You probably stunk."

I agreed, "I probably did, that place smelled nasty."

Gabe was staring at the minor scratch on my face. "Tara, you need to be careful doing this kind of shit. I hope you didn't bring anything home with you."

I breathed in through my teeth. "Well…"

My stepdad's eyes went wide. "Don't say it…I don't want to hear it!" He stood up and threw his hands in the air. "I'm going to go check to see if your car smells better. Come on, Austin." My brother moped the entire way out the door, he wanted to hear what I was about to tell my mom.

"And…" Mom was waiting for me to continue.

"Well, I was asleep, and I woke up to Bear standing over me staring at the door growling. He wouldn't let me get up to check it. Then when he finally relaxed, he laid his head on me. I tried to get up, but he growled at me. I went to sleep and nothing else happened."

Mom looked surprised but not scared. She was always the skeptic. "Wow, I really hope it was nothing, or Gabe is going to be a bundle of nerves."

We laughed at that thought.

I stood, "I'm going to get dressed to hang out with Jose and his family today."

"Okay, have fun." She held up her hand to stop me. "Oh, wait, what time will you be back later?" Gabe, Austin and I are going to San Antonio to do a little shopping, and we'll probably grab some food while we're out. Want me to bring you food back?"

I bit my inner cheek as I thought about the day. "I

don't know yet, but I'll get some food. Don't worry about me."

After getting dressed, I swiped my mom's keys from the counter since my car still had a tinge of stinky skunk to it. Gabe wouldn't let me drive it, he said in a day or two it would be fine. Again, worry-wart.

While I drove to Jose's my phone rang, it was mom. "Tara, where are you?"

"I'm on my way to Jose's. What's up?"

"Uhh...nothing, I was just making sure you left."

She said bye and hung up, weird.

I spent all day with Jose and his family; it helped take my mind off of the craziness going on. We didn't talk about the tour, and I needed that. His family ended up barbecuing, and I ate with them. By the time I got home it was early evening. My mom had texted me saying they'd be home later than they thought. They had stopped at my uncle's to visit for a bit.

I got home and my dogs all greeted me the way they usually did; I was glad things were back to normal with them. Everything seemed to be right again. Thank goodness. After letting Bear and my mom's dog out, I sat outside for a bit enjoying the pleasant breeze. I watched the beautiful sunset until it was dark out.

After a shower, I sat and scanned through the channels, but nothing seemed to catch my attention. Finally, giving up on that, I did a little schoolwork in my room. Bear followed me and laid on my bed as I worked. We had been sitting there quietly, when my tv turned on. It was snowy, and it turned the static sound all the way up. I reached around myself for the remote, maybe I had rolled on top of it. When it was nowhere under me, I realized it was sitting on my nightstand. I reached over and switched it off and set the remote back down. *That was weird.*

I went back to my homework. Bear was sitting on my bed staring at the tv, he did not like what just happened. Another ten minutes went by, and my television turned on again. Bear lost it this time. He stood over me and barked again. I grabbed the remote to turn it off once again. Getting up, I unplugged the damn thing from the wall. Now that should stop it.

While I walked back to my bed, I heard my family getting home. What a relief. I hurried out of my room and greeted them in the kitchen. I didn't tell them about the tv. Now that everyone was home, my nerves felt a tad bit better. I sat on the couch to watch a movie with Gabe and Austin, as my mom went to shower.

We were watching tv when we heard my mom yelling for Gabe. He jumped up and ran to their restroom. I sat on the edge of the couch waiting for him to come back.

When Gabe walked back in, his face was pale. "Tara, I hate to ask this because I really do not want the answer, but did you bring something home with you?"

I stood, "What happened?" Before he could reply I took off to their restroom. "Mom, what happened?"

She was wrapped in a towel, but she didn't look as upset as I expected her to be. "I was showering, and I felt something touch my chest. I looked out around the curtain expecting Gabe, and there was no one there."

I was pissed, "It touched you? What the hell!"

Mom brushed through her hair. "I think you brought something back with you. Earlier after you left, I was getting dressed, and I could have sworn you were in your room talking. That's why I called you. When you told me you had left, I walked to your room, there was no one in there and your tv was off."

Her call made much more sense now. "That explains the weird call."

She looked sheepishly back at me. "I didn't want to tell you and ruin your day. I thought it was just me and paid it no mind until this happened."

Welp, I guess I should come clean about the television turning on in my room now. "Before y'all got home, my tv turned on a few times. I had to unplug it. I didn't want to scare y'all, so I wasn't going to say anything."

She sat her hairbrush on the counter and turned toward me. "I'd rather know than not know, Tara. I feel like I'd be better prepared for what could happen."

I stared down at the laminate feeling upset with myself, she's right. "I'm sorry."

Mom patted my shoulder. When I looked at her, she was smiling at me softly. "It's okay, but tell me next time, please."

I agreed and left the room so she could get dressed. That night I went to bed fully expecting for something to happen, but it never did. I wasn't exactly put at ease, to be honest, it made feel like I needed to be more on guard. Whatever this was had to be toying with me. It wanted me to be caught off guard, and I would not give it that pleasure.

Before I fell asleep, I decided it was time to talk to it. "Alright, first of all, this is my house and you are not welcome here. Leave my family alone. Go back to the hospital. We do not want you here."

Maybe I was expecting something big to happen, like my door to open and close, a light switching, or something spiritual, but nothing. That night I went to sleep, and I slept peacefully, maybe it left? Guess only time will tell.

Chapter Three

To my surprise, and relief, the next couple of months were quiet, and nothing happened at all. Everyone seemed to be happy to have the house back to ourselves again. One night we had just gotten back from my little brother's football game, and we all went to our rooms to go to bed. It was a school night and I crawled into bed, I was about to drift to sleep, when I heard my door knob jiggle. Bear jumped up and started barking at the door. I managed to get up this time and open it. When I looked on the other side, there was no one there. I closed it, maybe it was Austin messing with me. Getting back into bed, I coaxed Bear to lie down. I fell asleep while running my hand through his fur.

I don't know how long I was asleep but was awoken to my bed shaking. I jumped out of the bed. It was still moving, but nothing else was shaking around the room. Bear was losing his mind barking. My door flew open behind me and I went into a defensive position, but it was only Gabe.

He looked like he was ready to kill. "I heard Bear, is everything okay?"

I lifted my hand and pointed at the bed. "My bed was shaking. I got up and nothing else was moving."

Mom walked into my room as I was telling my stepdad about what happened. "That's it, I'm buying prayer candles and putting them in every single room."

They were reluctant to leave me, but they knew that if anything else happened, Bear would alert them. I had to admit, I was a little nervous to lay back down, but I brought whatever this was home, and I needed to deal with it. Through the night, my bed would shake off and on, but I ignored it. I couldn't act on this. If I didn't acknowledge it, it would stop.

The shaking stopped eventually, and I could finally sleep. The next morning, I woke up groggy, but got dressed and went to school. When it was over, I hung out with Rachel for a bit before going home. As much as I loved my home, it had now become a place I hated being in. I hung out with my best friend until I had to go home, begrudgingly made my way back to my house of hell. When I walked in, mom was sitting on the couch still dressed in her scrubs. She was holding the remote in her hands like she was about to use it in battle.

What happened this time? "Mom, is everything alright?"

She peered over at me as I walked into the living room, "This damn thing you brought with you kept changing the channels on me. I would put it on something and then it would change. This went on about four times until I had enough. I told it to stop, and it did."

My mom is a pretty tough person, and I was proud she put her foot down. "That's good. We need to ignore it or establish that this is our home, and it's not welcome."

She nodded in agreement. "Yup, but this thing really needs to go, Tara."

I felt awful that I brought this thing home with me in the first place. This spirit had been in our house long enough, I couldn't live this way anymore, no one could. Since I brought it, I needed to get rid of it. The only question was how. How do I get rid of an unwanted attachment? Maybe if I did some research I could figure it out.

After I changed, mom let me know that they were going out. She asked me a few times if I wanted to go with them, but I told her no, I was fine. I definitely wasn't, but this was my chance to research how to get rid of it. They left later that evening, and as much as I didn't want to, I went to my room. Shutting the door behind me, I locked it as well. For some reason, that made me feel safer.

I had been scouring the web for hours when I heard walking sounds in the hallway. As I listened, I heard doors opening then closing. One by one, the doors in the hallway did this. Bear was standing by the door, hair raised and growling. My heart dropped when my doorknob moved. It started as a light shake and then got more aggressive when it couldn't get it open. Bear barked, and it stopped. In the corner of my closet I had an old bat leaning against the wall. I picked it up; I gripped it tightly with one hand as I reached to unlock the door with the other. I unlocked it and yanked it open. I grasped the bat with my other hand; I was ready to hit whoever it was on the other side of the door.

To my disdain, there was no one there. This torment had made me so miserable that I screamed down the hallway. "THAT'S IT! I'M DONE WITH THIS SHIT! You have taken my solitude, you've taken my happiness away! LEAVE NOW!!!! If you don't, I will force you."

If this thing didn't believe me, I was going to make it. I

grabbed the lighter on my nightstand and lit the candle mom had put in my room. As I went in and out of each room lighting the candles, I said every prayer I had learned. By the time I had made it to the kitchen, I was on the last prayer I could recall. Not sure if I said all the words right, but it would have to do. Once every candle was lit, the house felt less heavy.

Mom would kill me for falling asleep with all these candles on tonight, but I'm sure I could get a pass once I told her what happened. I woke up to my family getting home sometime in the night, and sure enough, mom wasn't happy. She didn't wake me though; Gabe must have come to my rescue. I silently thanked him and went back to sleep.

The next day I had to get out of the house. I went to my grandparents' house to visit with them for a bit. I hadn't been there long when I got a call from Gabe telling me to come home now. He sounded scared to death, so I rushed home.

When I got there, he and Austin were at the back patio waiting for me. "What's wrong? What happened?"

Gabe shows every emotion on his face and he looked pretty shaken up. "Tara, you need to get rid of this thing. Austin and I were sitting in the living room, and in my peripheral I saw something going down the hallway. I'm not saying that this is what it is, but I think it was a nun. I didn't want to scare Austin, so I made an excuse and we got out of there quickly."

I shook my head. "Where is mom? Is she still in there?"

He looked at me like I was crazy to ask that. "Of course not, I wouldn't have left her in there, Tara. She went to the store to get some groceries."

I felt silly asking him that, he would have never left her inside. He is one of the most protective people I know.

"I will get rid of it." I walked inside, and the house no longer felt light, it was back to feeling heavy. One by one I lit the candles and prayed.

Once I got the house feeling better, Gabe and Austin came back in. Mom got home, and he told her about what he had seen. Thankfully, Austin said he hasn't had anything happen to him at all. I wanted it to stay that way. He was a kid and didn't need to deal with any of this.

As we sat down to eat, I told them about the research I have done. I explained to them why I was leaving the candles on and that I was praying as I lit them. "The only thing I can think that would help, is to go back to the hospital and leave it there."

Mom and Gabe weren't too keen on me going back, but they knew it was worth a shot. It wouldn't hurt to try. We collectively decided that tomorrow was the day, we were done living in this hell.

I went to sleep feeling a bit more confident now that there was a plan. I only hoped that it would stay when I got to the hospital.

Chapter Four

The next afternoon, my mom and I went to my grandparent's house for my grandmother to pray for me. She gave me some holy water and a rosary they had gotten when they went to a big church down farther south. My grandmother wanted me to come back when it was done so she could pray again.

After agreeing, I went home to prepare for the evening. Rachel said she was coming to get me, and we'd go together. It relieved me she would do this for me. The idea of going back to that place was nerve-wracking enough and going alone made me really uneasy. When she got to my house, the sun was going down. My family wished me luck, and we left. On the way, we talked about what I was going to do.

I watched the scenery go by as we drove. "I really don't know what to do or say. My grandmother mentioned the rosary, but I don't remember it all."

She glanced over at me confused. "So, you're going into this with no plan, really? I thought you said you had one!"

I felt like I was being scolded, but she was right. "I thought I did, too."

My best friend tapped the steering wheel as she thought. "Why don't you look up the prayers you don't know on your phone."

I chuckled to myself. "That's a good idea, and I should have thought of that. How was that not a thought?"

She grinned. "Because I'm the smart one."

I reached over and smacked her on the arm. "Shut it." I pulled up the prayers, so I was ready when we got there.

We finally made it back to the eerie hospital. It was pitch black outside, and it only made the building look more menacing. All I could think was that it looked like a scene in a scary movie, and I was about to get out and walk right up to it. My hands were sweating, and I wiped them on my jeans.

Rachel parked and peered over at me. "Do you want me to get out with you?"

I shook my head. "No, I want to do this alone."

I picked up the bag I had stored all the things in that my grandmother had given me. Rachel watched me get prepared. I knew she wanted to help me, but I was stubborn and she let me be.

I reached for the door handle and then gazed back at my best friend. "Thank you for coming with me."

She looked back at me. "Break a leg!"

We both laughed, and I got out of her car. I took in the imposing building in front of me. The surrounding air was cooler than it should have been. My body shuddered from the chill or maybe it was the fear.

After taking a calming breath, I trudged toward the building. I turned to look back at my best friend. She gave me a thumbs up. I could do this, and it needed to be done.

Once I made it to the steps in front of the hospital, I

sat the bag down and pulled out the rosary and the holy water. I had no clue what to do. Thinking back to the movies I had seen for some reference. In one they had made a salt circle for protection. Since I had no salt, I made a circle around me with holy water.

When I was done with the circle, I sat down cross-legged in the middle. I grasped the rosary in my hands and began to say the rosary. I was halfway through it when I noticed I could hear faint voices around me. I peered around, and no one was there. I kept going. I got through a few more prayers; the rosary takes a while to get through. The doors in front of me vibrated, but I ignored it and kept going.

I had no idea how long I had been there, my butt had gone numb already. I was on the last prayer finally. "...Through the same Christ our Lord. Amen."

I stood and wiped the dirt off my jeans. I held the rosary tightly in one hand and the holy water in the other.

"That's it, you need to stay here, you are not welcome in my home anymore. I know that I'm an easy target, but you can no longer stay attached to me. I do not want you to be my friend or whatever you think. It's time to move on, or stay here for all I care."

I went to step out of the circle and stopped. One of the long windows off the side of the doors caught my attention. When my eyes focused on it, there was a dark figure standing, peering back at me. I couldn't make out anything but the shape. Like Gabe had said, it seemed to look like a nun.

I closed my eyes as my brain shuffled back to the stories that the tour guide had told us. There were a group of nuns that founded the hospital. Could it have been one of them? When I opened my eyes and looked back, the dark mass was gone.

I felt confident that I had left her here and stepped out of the circle. I stuffed the items back into the bag and turned to go back to the car. Rachel's eyes flicked between me and the hospital a few times. Before I got into the car, I peered back at the desolate hospital. There was a part of me that felt sorry for all the souls stuck in there, but at the same time, I didn't want any of them attached to me.

"I hope y'all find peace one day." I doubt anything heard me, but I still wanted to end this on a positive note.

I opened the door and dropped into the seat. Rachel was almost vibrating in her seat waiting for me to tell her something.

I turned to my best friend and smiled. "It's done, I think. Before I left the circle, I saw a black mass that looked like a nun in the window next to the door. I hope she went back."

Rachel appeared hesitant. "Are you sure it was a nun, or could it have been something taking the form of a nun?"

This made me second guess myself. "Well, I guess I don't really know. Either way, it felt like I left it there."

"Okay, well let's hope the job is done." With that, she put the car in reverse and got us out of there.

We kept the conversations light on the way back to my house. Rachel dropped me off and my mom walked out with her keys in hand. I knew she wanted to go to my grandparents' house so my grandmother could pray over me again. I got into her car and we made our way to their house.

It didn't take long for my grandmother to pray, and we were back on our way home. Neither one of us said much on the drive. My mom pulled into the carport and turned the car off. I was about to get out when I felt my mom grasp my arm.

"Do you think you left it?" She said curiously.

I puffed my cheeks before I replied. "Yes, I believe I did."

She let my arm go. "Good."

We both got out of the car and toward the house. The dogs were running around us happily, that was a good sign. We walked in and set our stuff down. Gabe was waiting for us in the living room.

"How did it go?" He looked at me.

"I think I got rid of it. I saw something in one of the windows before I left. The dogs even came near me when we got home. They haven't done that in a while." I felt pretty sure it did not come back with me.

He seemed much better after hearing my reply. "Thank goodness."

My parents went to bed, and I got ready for bed myself. The night had really worn me out. Bear was waiting for me on my bed after I showered. As usual, I text Jose to let him know how it all went. He felt bad he couldn't go, but he had to work. The supernatural stuff really creeps him out, so it was better to have Rachel go, anyway.

It didn't take me long to fall asleep, and when morning came, I felt better. The energy in the house was lighter and felt happier again. This was something my entire family had been hoping for since I brought that thing home with me.

The months passed one after another with no more experiences for any of us. A year later, the ordeal we had gone through faded from our minds. It was now a thing of the past that we rarely thought about anymore.

It was Halloween, and I was out with Jose's family taking his little sibling trick or treating. By the time I made it home, my family was already in bed. As I showered, I

Chapter 4 • 111

thought about last Halloween and the events that occurred after. Relief washed through me knowing that I didn't put myself in a position like that again.

I got dressed and walked toward my room, the feeling of someone watching me made the hair on the back of my neck rise. I turned on my heel and looked back at the dark area of the house. I reached over and flicked the restroom light back on. My eyes slowly adjusted to the added light. I took a couple steps toward the living room and peered around. Nothing was there. My mind was playing tricks, I should have not let it wander back to last Halloween.

Shrugging it off, I turned off the light and started toward my room. I was almost to my room, and a black mass was standing in front of my door. My eyes went wide in terror. Before I could react, it came flying toward me. I went to scream but nothing came out. My feet felt glued to the floor and I couldn't move. The apparition stopped inches from my face.

It went from being a black mass to having a face. A withered lady was staring back at me, she opened her mouth and my world went black.

About Stephanie Hassenplug

Stephanie is a newish author that's busy trying to balance being a military wife and raising four daughters. It requires a lot of swearing, Red Bull, and patience. She enjoys writing, reading, K-pop, watching K-dramas, and napping as much as possible. Stephanie has been reading all her life, and decided to take a stab at writing.

Follow her on Facebook: https://www.facebook.com/stephanie.hassenplugauthor.1

Join her Facebook group: https://www.facebook.com/groups/421137921896517/

And on Amazon for upcoming releases: https://www.amazon.com/-/e/B07TXRN63S

Other books by Stephanie Hassenplug:

<u>God Academy</u>

Love & Rage

Dark Goddess Omnibus (In-work)

<u>Standalones</u>

Embers Of A Broken Heart

Specter's Inc.

BY: JENÉE ROBINSON

Ghost Level

To the cast of Ghost Adventures, thanks for the inspiration. And to Zak Bagans, thanks for always sending Aaron to the scariest places alone.

Chapter One

EVER

"Whose idea was it to go to this asylum?" I complain to Luca.

He lets out a breath but doesn't say anything, just adjusts his glasses on the bridge of his nose and runs a hand through his short brown locks. I study him for a moment as he taps away at his keyboard.

"Atlas, you know he thinks he's in charge. So, he picks the places and we follow," he finally states, looking up to me from his screen. "Are you scared?"

"Pssh, no," I say, tugging on my gloves, "it's the Sheffield Asylum for the Criminally Insane? Come on that just screams a headache to me." It's really a bad habit but they make me feel secure.

"How can you wear those all the time? Don't your hands get all sweaty and gross?" he asks. The tattoos on his arms only give me pause for a second. The nerdy badass look he has works but before I can answer, a husky voice rings out.

"Really Luca? We've been working with her for over a year and you just got the balls to ask her?" Bastian exclaims as he enters our little make-shift office, in the trailer the three guys share. "You can't just ask someone that!"

"It's fine, I've been wearing gloves over half my life; when I was little, I hated it but as the years passed and my power intensified, I got over it and kept wearing them. Do you know how annoying it is to have to clean a bathroom shower before I use it, so much scrubbing just so I don't get a glimpse of a person naked or worse," I say with a shiver.

The looks on their faces are priceless. Bastian is a well-built man, never missing a day to admire his reflection in the gym mirror, but even with that vain side, he is a big old softy with me. Grossing each other out is usually a game we save when we are hunting for ghosts, but the timing was perfect for today.

My gift is also a curse at times, no real way of controlling it. The gloves are a big help but if the memory is strong enough it will seep through. When I was younger and the visions first started up after I touched a library book, I was transported into the mind of the previous reader as she hid in a closet with the shouts of adults yelling on the other side. My parents thought I was possessed, taking me from therapists to priests trying to rid the evil from my soul, but it was Psychometry. After a few years of research, I found the term in an occult book I managed to pick up on one of our ghost hunts.

One snowy day when I was younger, I put mittens on and realized that when I grabbed the door knob to go outside I didn't get a flash and decided to wear gloves ever since. When I stopped complaining about my visions, my parents worried less that I was evil and didn't even question the gloves.

"Are you all ready for the asylum?" Bastian asks,

rescuing me from my thoughts, as well as to cover the awkward tension in the room.

"Who's not ready for a good ghost hunt? It's been too long in between jobs," Luca complains.

"It's been three days," I reply with an eye roll.

"If I could do this every night, I would."

"I like my sleep too much for all of that. What am I a fucking vampire? Nope. Sleeping during the day is not for me. I want to be up in the daylight."

At my statement, the two of them laugh.

"Come on, Luca, let's get the van loaded up before Atlas gets back. You know how crazy he gets when he's itching to seek out the spirits," Bastian says.

"Don't we all?" Luca questions as he gets up from the comfy chair he was just in.

I follow them out to the living room, it is littered with equipment from the check they did last night. I let out a yawn which Bastian notices.

"Ever, go lay down in my bed," he orders, pointing toward his closed door. "Even with all this high tech gear, Atlas relies on you the most. You are no good to us dead on your feet."

Doing the most adult thing I can think of, I stick my tongue out at him.

This only riles him up more and soon he's stalking over to me and, with ease, lifting me into his arms. There is no use in fighting, his strength is unmet by mine, so I just go with it.

"You aren't fighting, you must really be tired," Bastian remarks.

I don't reply right away because all the comments that come to mind would make this awkward and I don't want to test the close bond I have with the guys.

"Nah, what's the point? I'd never win and a nap sounds nice." I smile up at him.

He smirks at me as he kicks the ajar door open and lowers me onto his unmade bed. There are extra pillows next to me, so I grab one to snuggle with as he tucks me in. It's these sweet moments that sometimes make me yearn to be more than a friend or co-worker with any one of them, but I remind myself that we are a team and love and business do not always mix well.

"Spooky dreams," he whispers as he closes the door behind him.

I pay him no mind as I pull the pillow closer and drift off to sleep.

Atlas

"You ready, fuckers?" I ask as I return home from scoping out the location, this is the first one we've found so close to home and I've been dying to look inside since I was a kid. Sheffield Asylum is the place that we would dare our friends to get close to, but never go in. The rumors of that place were things that nightmares were made of, and I was a believer.

One run-in with a specter and I was hooked on finding more. The night that my mother died, I was holding her hand as she passed, and I swear that my grandmother smiled at me as she took my mom's hand, leading her into whatever happens to you after you die. From that moment, I knew what my calling was, finding and communicating with the dead, and it's still hard to believe that I'm living the dream.

"Almost got all the equipment in the van, Ever is napping and we will be ready to roll in no time," Bastian answers.

Raising an eyebrow at him, "Where exactly is she sleeping?"

His cheeks go a little pink at my question, "In my bed." He gives me a little shoulder shrug.

"Good, a quick nap isn't a bad idea for her. I know that those visions she gets drain her, so it's great that she is resting until we leave. What do you need me to load?"

"We are good, boss," Luca pipes in. "You make sure you have all your maps or whatever it is you need. Me and this big lug got the rest."

I give them a nod, "I'm going to peek in on Ever and then head to my office. If you change your mind, let me know."

I stop at Bastian's room. With gentle hands, I turn the knob and slightly open the door. There sprawled out on the bed is Ever, one leg out of the covers and but still nestled in the mass of pillows on the bed. I don't wake her, it is a rare sight that she is so at peace. The hell her visions put her through is unnerving and I don't even see what she does. I love that she is willing to use her gift for our team, but at times I regret it. Most of the places we travel to are filled with pain and grizzly murders, anger or sorrow seem to fuel the spirits not to cross over. So, this little slice of a calm Ever is heaven to my eyes.

I close the door with the same gentleness as I opened it and return to the guys, grabbing a load of equipment and heading to the van.

"Ever okay?" Bastian questions.

"Yes, I know these adventures make her a little restless, so it's great that she is sleeping soundly for a little bit. When we get there, I'll call the owners so we can chat for a few, getting what they have on the history from them as well as any of the experiences they've had at the asylum. They will clear the estate and then lock the gates until they come for us in the morning." I reply, oversharing information like I usually do.

Luca pipes in, "So, no chance of any hot chicks meeting up with us?"

Bastian and I both let out a laugh.

"Only the dead kind, brother," Bastian replies.

"One can only hope."

Chapter Two
———————

EVER

The crunch of the tires on the cobblestone road that leads up to the asylum sends a shiver running down my spine. A strong energy hit me as we rolled onto the grounds, the butterflies in my stomach were starting a little revolt. The closer we got to the asylum the faster they flew, causing bile to raise in my throat.

"Ever, are you okay?" Atlas asks, placing a hand on my shoulder for comfort.

I lazily lift mine to his before I reply, "Yes, just a little overwhelming. There's a lot of energy just hitting me from the grounds. I don't know if I'll be able to enter without spewing everywhere."

"That's good to know," Atlas replies, slowly removing his hand.

I can't help but laugh, as my words sink in. He is turning a little green himself, which makes me laugh a bit more. "I'm fine, I promise. I'll let you know if it gets worse and I need to jump out."

The tingling feeling of his hand on my shoulder touch helped more than his words but how can I express that without just blurting out my true feelings for him? Something about the guys has a soothing effect on me. But I'm not going to tell them that. *I'm not crazy, right?*

Milling around in my head and trying to hide away my feelings, I didn't notice the van come to a stop. Atlas's hand is once again on my shoulder but this time giving me a little shake.

"Ever, are you ready? The owners are standing outside the front door for their interviews." He pauses to let me answer, but I guess I take too long, "We gotta get going before it gets dark."

I turn towards him and give him a smile, "I'm always ready, let's do this."

He removes this hand once again and heads out the driver's side door. Just as I reach for the handle, the door is jerked open. A smirking Bastian is waiting on the other side, holding out a hand to help me down. If we were back in the 1700s, I might consider myself flattered.

"Thank you, Bastian," I say with a confused look on my face as the words tumble slowly from my mouth. I don't know what his deal is because he never does these sweet things for me. Honestly, it is a little freaky.

"Stop looking at me like I'm a psycho, I know this job has you on edge. So, I decided to try not to be an asshole, okay?" he says while rolling his eyes.

Cautiously I take his hand, eyeing him to make sure he is, indeed, my Bastian. After a long and hard once over, I am satisfied he isn't some doppelganger and I jump down from my seat.

"Sorry, you're being sweet, and I never see this side of you. I'm just a little weirded out." I confess with a shrug.

Bastian lets out an awkward laugh as we cross the lawn towards the couple standing near the front porch of the asylum. Once we reach them, Atlas has already started chatting with them. He introduces us as we come up the sidewalk with our gear in tow, stopping near him to give them a polite wave.

They both eye my gloved hands but smile when their eyes meet mine.

"As I mentioned on the phone this is our resident, psychometrer, Ever. Hopefully with her hands and visions, we can get some answers to what or who is haunting you guys."

They don't really say anything just nod as he moves on to Bastian. I gaze at the windows that line the first level of tonight's fun house. Don't get me wrong I love helping the dead move over to the other side, if I can, but most would rather stay and annoy the living. Maybe 'annoying' is too tame, 'piss off' would be more accurate. As my eyes reach the last frame, a black shadow passes behind the glass.

A shiver runs down my spine and I go a bit weak in the knees. Bastian notices as he hooks his arm around my waist for more support. He leans in, his warm breath tickling my ear, "They start already?"

I rest my head on his shoulder and nod on it.

Luca

Ever was extra quiet on the ride compared to normal, usually she joins in on the rundown of how the night will go, but not tonight. The other guys take notice, yet seem to shrug it off. They just roll on with the plans like nothing is different.

Atlas is all hyped up and some of his energy is starting to rub off on me. The nerves in my stomach are easing some and excitement is taking its place. "Is there any place that we aren't allowed?"

"Yes, the basement is out of bounds. It's in the worst shape, so for our safety we are steering clear of there."

"How many rooms and floors again?" Bastian asks.

"Geez, I'm going to start tattooing all the info on your forehead, maybe then you won't forget." Atlas laughs before answering his question, "Bastian, I want you to stick like glue to Ever's side in the asylum. There's no arguing about this, from either of you. This place is huge and we are buddying up. No one on their own, got it?"

Jealousy wells up in my chest that I wasn't picked to be Ever's buddy. If I speak up, then they will know I have a thing for her, right? *Will they? Maybe they will think I am just concerned because she gets so drained?*

I decide against it, as she appears the most relaxed as I've seen her in days. Even if it's on that cocky bastard's shoulder. I glance in their direction and he winks at me, not one to miss an opportunity. I return it with a mocking kiss, which gets an eyebrow raise from Ever. I note that her head shakes a little as Bastian chuckles.

"Ready?" Altas questions, "I want to scout before the sun sets and get all the equipment set and ready, so if there is any activity we are ready to roll."

Altas takes out the walkie talkies we have for when we split up and radios Bastian and Ever. "Bastian, I have a map here and have marked some points that I'd like you to set up the thermal cameras. You and Ever can handle that right?" I leave a pause before I continue, "There are also a couple of the hot spots in there that I want Ever to see if she can get some readings on. If it's too much on her, come back to the van for the night, these spirits are evil bastards. Right before nightfall, the owners are going to come back for a short interview...you know for that spooky effect."

"Only you, Atlas," I joke, shaking my head and

giggling to myself, "What...are our five followers going to enjoy that more?"

I can feel him rolling his eyes at me through the walkie talkies, "Get your ass inside. We have some ghosts to find."

"Aye, aye, Captain,' I reply, giving him a little salute as I skip up the few steps and take a pause before I cross the threshold. Once I am about a foot from entering the threshold, a cool forceful breeze hits me, almost knocking me back into someone. I look back and see it is Altas. *How did they get up here already?*

"Dude, you okay?" he asks, nudging me inside.

"Just a chill came over me. I should've brought a thicker jacket," I remark.

Why didn't she fucking bring her jacket. She knows she is colder the more she sees. *Why the fuck do I care? She is just a team member.*

"I knew this place would be a hotbed for the supernatural," his voice starts to get a high pitch because he is giddy.

Once we are both in, he takes the lead which I'm happy to hand over. He is practically skipping on the scuffed and worn checkered floor.

"Was this place always an asylum? I mean I know it's in the name but was it built just for that purpose?" I ask, before he disappears behind a wooden doorframe.

"Yes," his voice floats out towards me as I round the doorway.

He doesn't finish his statement until I'm right next to him. "It was built for that purpose alone. Some wacko doctors with their crazy cures, got state funding to house and treat the mentally unstable."

"More like torture them, you mean," I remark.

"Yes, that's what makes it perfect, revengeful spirits are usually the most active."

I glance around, the walls are hospital white where the paint isn't peeling from the sheetrock. The checkerboard floor is something out of the old horror movies I watched as a kid. Trying not to shiver as I think of the million horrible things that went down here, I follow behind him.

Chapter Three

EVER

It was sweet of Atlas thinking that I needed a babysitter, he took into account my unease, but I'm a grown-ass woman. He doesn't realize that I am the one that cares for them when they are freaking out. I don't want or need Bastian as a tag along. He is an asshole most of the time and also eye candy. I don't need that getting in my way as I try to concentrate and track the spirits that have been stuck here for close to a century.

"What's going on in that pretty little head of yours?" Bastian asks, following a mere few steps behind me.

I scrunch up my nose and just shake my head at him.

"You were wandering around here and ignoring me calling your name, so spill, were you thinking about me?" He smirks, holding up the camera that is slung around his neck as if to take a picture of my reaction.

Schooling my features, hoping he can't read between the lines, I answer, "Why would *you* be on my mind?"

His lips fall into a frown, "Well..."

Before it can get any more awkward in there, I ask him for the map. It's more of a rough stretch than anything, and the chicken scratch of Atlas's labels to what each room is, is barely legible. "We are supposed to use this as a guide in this monstrous place? I can't tell where we even are on this thing."

"Why do you think I shoved it in my pocket. I gave it a once over when Atlas handed it to me." He shrugs, "It's useless, we do need to stick together, so when we get lost, we aren't alone."

"When?" I throw my head back and laughter erupts from my throat, "Always the optimist, aren't we?"

His lips turn up into a little smirk at my words. "Maybe....places that are this big can be hard to navigate, so what I see in the future is we are lost and looking for a way out."

"Well, before we get lost, do you need a hand with those cameras? I can help, you know."

He shakes his head, "Nah, I got this. If you want to follow me and pick up things I may drop, though, I would appreciate that. Atlas told me that the places that will have the most activity are on the first floor. So, we will help in the dining hall, the living room—aka the group therapy room—and the hydrotherapy room. Then we can come back out for the spirit boxes and the digital records."

At the mention of hydrotherapy, a shiver tingles down my spine. I must pale even more as he continues to talk because the moment he stops, he is by my side in a flash, supporting me. The equipment all hits the floor with a dull thud.

"Bastian, I'm fine. Hydrotherapy gives me the creeps is all. The mere thought of the flashes I will get in there has me a little on edge. This is why I didn't want to come here. I'm not a big water lover as is, so the thought of a memory of someone drowning is not high on my list of 'want to see'." I try to play it off as a joke, but he sees right through me.

He lets go of me, his warmth leaving me with another chill and heads to pick up everything he dropped.

"You don't have to go in; if you want, you can wait at the door while I set up the camera. These spirits are going to wreak havoc with you once they know what you can do. I think that's why you are already dreading this hunt, Atlas may not believe me, but ghosts can sense when someone is more in tune with them than normal. And maybe on some level, he does, because this is the first time we have been paired up together. I mean, I'm not complaining but I bet Luca is."

His last sentence catches me off guard, "What...what do you mean 'Luca is'?"

Bastian remains silent.

"Oh no, you can't just drop a bomb and forget it went off. Spill it," I say, as I make my way over to him, I don't stop until his back is on the wall.

"Easy there, Killer, it was just a slip of the lips. Forget I said anything."

"I will not, but we can discuss this later, Atlas will have our heads if you don't get these cameras set up."

Why would Luca want to be paired with me?

"You're not wrong, now can you back up a little bit?" He smiles.

I had forgotten that I had him pinned to the wall. My cheeks flush a little as I take a step back from him. He quickly gathers up the equipment and then I follow him towards our first target. Just awkward silence hangs between us as we trudge deeper into this worn torture house.

"For it always being an asylum they have a weird set up. Where are all the double doors to lock the patients in? I can't imagine that they would just let them roam freely if they were criminals and insane," I mutter to Bastian.

"I was wondering the same thing. Doing a little digging on this place verifies there were murderers enhoused here, how in the world would they just run free? This place doesn't make any sense," he replies before stopping down the long corridor in front of the broken wooden door. "Does this look like a living room to you?"

I step up beside him and peek through the shards of wood. There are what may be sofa under white sheets and a few tables with chairs around them.

"Only one way to know for sure." I shrug. "But how do we get in? This door will fall off its hinges the moment we try to open it. I wonder if there are another set of doors at the other end?"

"Smart thinking, I knew Altas saw more to you than a pretty face and a spooky gift." Bastian winks.

"Ha ha, why's he need you then?" I retort, a smirk tipping my lips.

He raises a hand over his heart and says, "Ouch, that hurts right here."

The smile leaves my face as a black shadow floats from one door frame into another, a mere few feet ahead of us.

"D-did you see that?" I ask Bastian, blinking my eyes, halfway hoping that it was just my imagination.

"What? What did you see?" he questions me.

"Maybe it was just a trick of the light. Yeah, that's what it has to be. Forget I said anything," I reply, waving him off.

"One thing I know from adventures like this, when you see something, it's there whether I see it or not. So, take a deep breath and talk to me."

Following his orders, I inhale and exhale slowly and look deep into his chestnut eyes. "There was a black shadow just there," I say, pointing to where I saw it. "The form was taller than you, thin and all black. Almost as if it was smoke coming from under the doorway."

"It's insane that we are having some activity already. We need to document that form and get these cameras up asap," Bastain says, the excitement in his voice has his deep bass almost up to a baritone.

My breathing is a little heavier and my heart is thumping like a drum but I follow wordlessy behind him. Normally, they are the ones cowering in fear, so I have to suck up these emotions and get the job done. The name of this place has just seeped into my brain and is playing tricks on my nerves. Not one of our journeys has gotten under my skin like this place, but I will take back ownership and show these spirits who's boss.

Bastian drops the bags he is carrying and begins digging through them for the thermal camera and all the goodies that go with it, while I work on getting the door open. Where the other one was in pieces this one has held tight. The handle turns in my grip but the door doesn't budge. I decide that leverage may work to get it to move and my shirt flits up as I use my hip to get the wooden door to open. It launches me not only inside but into the past.

Bastian

"Ever, Ever…!" I scream frantically as she molds to my arms; she is like Jello if I try and move her into a more comfortable position. When she crashed through the door and hit the floor, I lost my shit.

Think, dumbass, she must be having a vision. There isn't anything you can do for her until she comes back to the land of the living. So, like the idiot I am, I just hold her. With a gentle hand I push back the hair that had feathered on her face from the jostle of me pulling her into my lap.

Once I make sure Ever's in a comfortable position, I grab my cell from my pack and dial Atlas.

"All set already? You must be as excited as I am for this hunt tonight," Atlas chirps on the other end after only one ring.

"We've had a little set back with Ever," I reply, not able to contain the nervousness in my tone.

"What?" He screams into the phone.

"Bro, calm down. She's been pulled into a vision. This place must have a lot of activity or a strong connection with her." I tell him, as I glance back down to check her breathing. "As soon as she comes around, I will finish setting up the camera. She had been a little hesitant to enter the asylum but she is a trooper. Are you sure this is a good idea? I mean I'm down, but it seems to already be taking a toll on Ever."

"Nut up, she knew what she signed up for. Luca and I went up to the second floor. We will come back down in a few once we have dropped some of this gear off. Next time, use your walkie, that's what they are for, rookie." His side goes dead as he hangs up before I can get a word in.

"Fuck that asshole," I mutter, pocketing my phone. Mister high and mighty, but when it comes down to it, who does he send into the most haunted or tragic space? Me. That's who. He's worried he will piss in his khakis on camera. That pussy.

My anger subsides some as Ever stirs. I can't take it out on her, Atlas just knows how to rub everyone the wrong way. And like an asshat, he does it just because he can.

"Welcome back, Ever. You good to sit up?" I wait for her to nod and push up before I continue talking. "I'll get a video camera ready and you can retell your vision. Atlas and Luca will be here in a little bit. So, you can wait until they are here or just get started. Fucking Atlas is too giddy about this place. Sometimes, I want to punch him in the face."

"Well, now don't get all emotional on me. Bastian. May start thinking there is a heart under that playboy exterior," Ever teases me with a wink.

I can't keep the smile from my lips at her words. 'Playboy', ha. If only she knew. This ghost hunting gig doesn't get us nearly as many girls as she thinks. We are labeled hot nerds and not all women are into that. I grab the handycam and hand it to her before digging for the thermal one I have to set up for the night.

Once I have all the pieces of the tripod and camera, I glance around the room for the best vantage point to get a good view of any activity. This room is huge, I better got a second camera set up. Ever didn't wait on Altas and Luca, the whispers of her tale reach me on this end of the room.

I decide that one camera will go up under the box TV that is mounted on the wall, out of the reach of the patients. The other will go close to the doors where we came in. The sound of footsteps nears us. Stepping out to meet them, I find Altas has a smile plastered on his smug face but Luca is following behind in his shadow as if something will jump out and grab him.

"What happened to Ever?" Atlas demands, glancing down the corridor.

"Too much spiritual energy knocked her into a vision. I panicked a little because I've never seen it hit her so hard. She's recording it all now and I have two cameras set up and ready. I have two more rooms to go. If you want to stay here with Ever, I'll head down and get them up and running."

Luca pipes in a little too fast, "I will."

"Chill those hormones, bro, or are you just scared of this place?" I tease him.

He gives me the finger, then he pushes past me to check on Ever.

"I have to get camera-ready for the interviews, you okay rigging those up by yourself?" he asks, fluffing his ice-white hair a bit.

"Fuck, yes. I'm not a toddler that needs my hand held. Are you confusing me with Luca again?"

For the first time since we arrived, his stance eases and he smirks and turns towards the first doors to go primp. Really? 'Camera ready'? Does he need to fix his makeup or something? Since I've known him, there's never been one stray hair on his perfect, fat head.

Ducking back in, I notice that Luca is talking with Ever. Most likely about her vision, my curiosity is piqued but there is shit to do first. I ignore them as they chat away and grab my gear, heading back into the spooky-ass hall to find the next two rooms we are to film in.

Chapter Four

EVER

"Luca, I'm fine, really." I smile, trying to reassure him. "This place is full of the dead, so many spirits in one place are a little more overwhelming than the normal haunts we frequent."

"Are you sure?" His voice is full of concern and he lightly touches my arms.

Is he joking right now? I have bigger balls than the three of them combined. Why is he questioning me now?

"Yes, I'm good to go. Where's Bastian heading off to? I thought we were supposed to stay in pairs?"

"He and Atlas were still outside the room when I came to check on you. I'm sure they are setting up the other cameras, is there anything else that you need to set up?" Luca askes, giving me a wide smile, and I can swear there is a glint off his pearly whites.

"I think I'm ready. Just feel bad that I didn't help Bastian set up like it was planned," I confess.

"Ever," my name rolls off his tongue a little too smoothly. He steps a little closer and puts my face up with a finger under my chin until my gaze falls on his. "He was so freaked when you fell into a vision. I could hear the shake in his voice and I wasn't on the phone. You mean more to us than you realize."

"Luca," a muffled voice calls.

He turns away from me, but grabs my hand at the same time to pull me with him.

"Luca, come help me with the interview with the caretakers," Atlas demands, a smug smile on his face.

Atlas adores the spotlight, if he wasn't chasing ghosts, his cheekbone structure would have him in modeling. He has himself convinced that he was made to be in front of the camera. I mean, don't get me wrong he is hot; but damn, sometimes he's too insufferable.

"Sure, want Ever to come with us?" Luca asks, his tone light.

"Nah, if she wants to go find Bastian and help him that would be good. Lockdown will start as soon as we complete the interviews."

Trying to hold the eye roll, I nod and let loose of Luca's hand. "I'll head and find Bastian. Have fun with the interviews."

I control my breathing as a cold breeze passes through me, just glad it didn't knock me into another vision. This hallway seems to go on forever, I hope that I can find Bastian soon. Some of the energy in here is not the good kind. Evil even. I can't imagine the horrors that took place behind these closed doors and I know some of them will plague me later worse than the first one I had. The best part of that one was waking with Bastian holding me. Most guys are freaked out by my gifts, for him not to recoil from touching me was a nice change.

"Bastian, come out, come out wherever you are," I call, my voice echoing down the hall.

The checkered tiles creak louder with each step, making me question the integrity of the baseboards. Why do ghosts have to haunt all the broken-down places? Just for once, can we investigate a posh hotel? I'll have to bring that up at the next meeting.

I am also at the end of the hall when my name is whispered in my ear on a cold breath. Goose bumps spread down my body as I refuse to stop until I get to the last door and poke my head inside.

"Bastian, there you you." My tone is more of a scowl than a statement. "Need any help?"

He looks up from the camera he just set on the tripod. "Nope, this was the last one. Why are you walking around here by yourself? Who's ass do I need to kick?"

I can't stop the laugh that escapes. "What is up with you and Luca? If I didn't know better I'd think you two are crushing on me."

His cheeks flush and now I am questioning if I was right.

Bastian shrugs. "What if I am?"

The careless way he asks, I can't tell if he is joking or not.

"We are ready to roll, any more activity on your way to find me?"

"One cold spot and a whisper of my name, but other than that, no visions. I did keep my hands to myself," I say, wiggling my fingers in my gloves. "Shouldn't be long till show time. Ready to head back out front and see if Altas has had enough of hearing his own voice yet?"

This time Bastian is the one laughing. "I'm glad that I'm not the only one that's noticed that."

He grabs his bags and leads the way back to the front. We make it about halfway before he stops and I bump into him. My hands grip the hard muscles of his back, when I realize I'm holding on to him, I drop my hands fast to my sides.

"You okay?" I whisper.

"Did you hear that?" he replies, thin lipped.

"No, what did you hear?"

"A female voice with my name on her lips."

"This is about the same spot where I heard my name, but it was a male voice." I step up next to him and pat his shoulder. "Always freaky when they call us by name. Do you need to go change your shorts before we lock down?"

"Seriously, Ever? You had to go there?" His nose is scrunched in disgust.

"Come on, let's find the other two. They think they're the rockstars of this adventure, but we are the real ones, aren't we?" I say, bumping my shoulder into his.

"You're damn right, we are."

Finally, his smile has returned to his beautiful face. Before he starts moving, he takes my hand in his and pulls me along. The act of comfort is one I don't normally welcome, but he needs it just as much as I do.

This place is scary as fuck and that's saying a lot coming from the girl with visions.

Just as we hit the threshold, Atlas's voice booms in, why did it take until today for me to realize how full of himself he really is?

Bastian

I couldn't believe that Ever accepted my hand, but the scowl on Luca's face when he saw us come through the door was icing on the cake. When I told him I thought I was falling for her, he confessed the same. We both agreed that we wouldn't push ourselves on her but let her decide if she was interested in either of us. Technically, I just took her hand and she didn't reject me, so he can't be mad. Right?

When we make it up to the front of the asylum, Atlas is shaking hands with the caregivers.

"Thanks again for letting us ghost hunt here tonight," Atlas calls to them as they are walking back to their car before turning back to us, with a creepy, wide smile on his lips. "Are you guys ready? I'm so pumped to get back in there. Luca and I got a few cold spots when we were on the second floor. That doesn't count whatever you and Ever ran into."

"I hit a cold spot in the hall, a male voice whispered my name, and I had a vision, but I'll tell you guys about that later. Bastian heard a female voice, too. This place is full of energy, I didn't even take my gloves off and I was hit with a vision, I've never had that happen before. This place is legit," Ever confirms, squeezing my hand a little at the same time.

"Well, let's get this party started. Ever and Bastian will start with a spirit box in the living room. If she was pushed into a vision without touching anything, I bet that it will be a hot spot for spirits. Radio us if the site goes dry and move on to the dining room, but I want you to wait for us before the hydrotherapy room. If there are ghosts in there, they are angry and maybe vengeful, so we have to choose our words carefully," Atlas warns.

"Where are you and Luca going?" Ever asks.

"Back to the second floor, we found a couple of doctors' offices as well as the head nurse's. Luca and I agree that when the riot happened some of the patients probably went up there to have their revenge. So, we are having to get some digital recordings of either the doctors or patients, fingers crossed we have lots of evidence of this haunting. Once we cut all the tapes together maybe we will finally go viral," Atlas states.

"Viral or not, we have the best job in the world," Luca chirps in, moving a little closer to Ever.

"Getting paid to do this would be great, too, though. I like having a roof over my head," Ever comments.

"Fame and fortune, that's my plan." Atlas beams.

The three of us sigh, and roll our eyes.

"Let's get going, we are burning night time. The ghosts are ready to play," I tell them.

"They've waited years, they'll wait a little longer. I want to grab my coat, I have a feeling that it's going to be a chilly night," Ever says, slipping her hand out from mine and heading toward the van.

"I'm a little worried about this hunt with Ever. She didn't even take her gloves off and had a vision." Luca is expressing the same concern I have.

Atlas sighs this time as he pinches the bridge of his nose. "You two need to stop thinking with your dicks. She is a big girl, if she didn't want to join in on this hunt, she would've told me. She is here of her own free will. I teamed her up with Bastian because he is good at reading people, he will know if it's getting to be too much for her and get her out. I'm not the heartless bastard you two think I am; plus, I'm not blind to see the pair of you have a thing for her. Let's try and keep it professional. What you three do on off hours, I don't care, but don't bring it to work. If I wasn't so into my work, I'd throw my hat into the ring. Ever is something special and not just because she's gifted."

"I don't think it's just the two of us," I mutter, and when I meet Atlas's gaze, the flush on his cheeks confirms I'm right.

Ever jogs up beside Atlas and places a hand on his shoulder, "What are you guys talking about?"

"Just about the basement, wondering if it really is as bad as the owners claimed." The lie slips too easily off Altas's tongue, making me question what other things he's fibbed to us about.

"Ever, are you ready?" I ask, ignoring Altas's statement. "The ghosts seem excited to have us here."

Shit, do I sound like an excited teenager?

"As ready as I'll ever be," Ever answers.

"After you," I say, motioning for her to go ahead.

"Sure, send me in first. Always the gentlemen, huh?" She rolls her eyes as she walks ahead of me.

A small laugh escapes my lips as I follow behind her.

Once we are back inside, after turning on her flashlight, Ever turns to me, "So, you have the spirit box? I have a digital recorder in my pocket."

She palms her front jean pocket and pulls out the little device. "Let's try a few EVPs and then we can work with the box. That thing is too loud to run to the whole time. Gives me a headache."

"Sounds good to me. Ghosts, come out, come out wherever you are," I call.

"Don't taunt the spirits," Ever says as she playfully slaps my arm.

This time, she takes my hand and leads me to the living room, her steps slow as we near the door.

"I'm here," I try to reassure her as she goes ahead and steps in.

Regretfully, I take my hand from hers. "Can you start that camera? And I'll grab the other and we will be ready for some EVP sessions."

She gives me a thumbs up before I head to the camera.

It only takes me a moment to switch the camera on and make sure it's on night-mode.

"Ever, want to meet me in the middle of the room? We can start here and work our way around the room? I want you to do most of the talking. When this place was open, it had mostly female nurses, so I think they will respond to you."

"Fine, but if we don't make any contact, you have to do the spirit box," she counters.

"Deal!"

"Turn off your flashlight and I will get started," Ever tells me.

The click of our flashlights is the only sound in the room. I point my handy-cam at her then when Ever starts talking into her recorder, I stay quiet and listen to her work. Making sure to video the exchange.

"Who's in this room?"

She pauses as we wait to see if anyone answers.

….Joseph…. a male voice whispers.

"Oh, did you hear that?" Ever asks, excitement in her voice.

"Yes, Joseph, I think," I reply.

"Did you die here?"

….murdered….

"Yikes, I heard murdered!" I exclaim. "Keep going."

"Who murdered you?" Ever asks.

….Dr…...Hurt….

"Wow, this is crazy. We've never gotten so many class-A EVPs in one room, let alone so close together or in the same room," Ever proclaims eagerly.

"I don't think we need to use the spirit box, we are getting good footage with digital recorders. What do you think?" I ask Ever.

BANG

"What was that?" I ask.

"I don't know, have to wait for a playback and see if we can find any movement or anything."

The walkie on my hip fills with Atlas's voice. "Upstairs is a bust, we are heading to the hydrotherapy room. Meet us there."

Chapter Five

EVER

Bastian and I click on our flashlights at the same time, two tiny streams of light guide us to the doors we entered when out of nowhere, a disembodied voice says, "Don't go."

The hair on the back of my neck is standing on end.

"Did you hear that?" I ask Bastian as I place a hand on his arm.

"What the fuck? We didn't even have the digital recorder going to catch that. This place is like a gold mine for EVPs. But why would it tell us not to leave?"

"I'm going to turn on my digital recorder and ask. Atlas can hold his horses, if not he can answer to me," I say as I pull the electronic device back out of my pocket as I turn off my flashlight.

"Why can't we leave?"

Silence.

....Dr. Hurt....

"Is he still here?" I ask.

....Danger....

"Does he want to hurt us?"

….Likes pain….

"Dr. Hurt likes to hurt people?"

I look in Bastian's direction, he comes to stand a little closer, his body heat warming me a little. Gah, now is not the time to think about how close he is, and I wish he was closer.

….Yes….

"I don't know, Bastian. Do you think we should go to the hydrotherapy room? This spirit, Joseph, just told us he was murdered and Dr. Hurt means to harm us," I ask, confliction in my tone.

Bastian doesn't answer, he clicks on his flashlight and grabs the walkie from his side.

"Atlas," he says into the little plastic box.

Silence,

"Atlas," he calls again.

More silence.

….Hurt got him….

"Fuck, Joseph, you could've said that sooner!" Bastian exclaims as he grabs my hand and pulls me from the room. "We need to find them."

The thunder of our feet on the squeaking tiles is like a herd of elephants as we rush to the room that I have been dreading this whole time.

Bastian slows us down as we make it to the doors to the room. I'm one step in when my vision blurs and I'm falling face-first into a vision.

When I awaken, I am freezing and my teeth are chattering so hard that I am starting to get a headache. Taking in my surroundings, I am in the hydrotherapy room and worse I'm in one of the chambers. The nurses have me submerged in chilly water with only my head in the cutout of the cover of the tub.

"Welcome back, Miss Hoffman, are you ready for your next session?" This menacing, handsome man is walking toward me, the electric wires sparking in his hands.

The last thing I hear is the bloodcurdling scream coming from my throat as my vision goes black.

To be continued....

About the Author

Jenée Robinson has been married for 19 years now, has three ornery girls, and lives on a cattle farm.
Writing has always been one of her loves and she's excited to see where it takes her. She has one trilogy of novellas complete and book one of her Arthurian done and several more out.
She has completed several short stories, and has more releasing soon. She is busy writing more, as well as more novellas and books.
Other than writing, she loves reading and photography. She's a Harry Potter Nerd and loves the show Supernatural and Captain America.

Also By Jenée Robinson

The Creeper Saga
Fate of the Fate

Curse of the Fae

Redemption of the Fae

Couldn't Keep Her

Polymorphic Passion

Sword of Ages
Legend of the Stone

Descendants of Nightmares
Academy of Monsters

The Monster in Me

The Hunt

Stalker's Path

Hunter

Seeking Their Souls

Goddess of Storms

Making Friends

BY: C.L. THORNTON

Ghost Level

Jared,
Thank you for your service to our country.
Thank you for being the kind of man I always dreamed of.
Thank you for being the kind of man our girls want to grow up and marry,
The kind of man our sons will grow to be. For always putting us first.
Love,
Your Jerk

Chapter One

Footsteps come up behind me quickly and I freeze. It's bad enough that I'm walking home from work because my sister forgot to pick me up. Again. But now I am rushing down the path to my house wondering when am I going to get knocked down. I have been hearing the sounds of someone following me for the past thirty minutes. I don't look behind me because I don't need the person to know they have me frightened.

I stand tall making sure to put my keys between my fingers like my dad taught me. I regret not grabbing the mace he gave me for Christmas. My dad being a Marine wanted his girls prepared for anything. Of course, I was the middle girl and did what I wanted. Which meant I didn't pack the mace in my purse because 'I would never need that'. Instant regret now though. I just want to make it to twenty-one. I know I can do it. I am determined to show this stalker my kick-ass moves. I will make him or her eat my fist! My best friend is a guy who stands at six foot seven. He has always made me spar with him so I am ready.

Suddenly stopping I spin around prepared to take on the asshole who is getting me all worked up. Only there is no one there. Hmmm. Okay, I am starting to get to myself obviously. Damn me and my fascination with scary movies. I just made myself the dumb blonde who gets dicked and then killed. The best part is… it's all in my head. Turning back around to finish the walk home I almost run right into the young girl. She looks about twelve and shouldn't be out at this time of night. Her hair is a mess and there are twigs in it. She is just standing in the walkway smiling at me. I can't help but look around just in case this is a ploy and some man is going to jump out and try to snag me. Scary movie fanatic remember?

"Hey there. You okay? You lost?" Duh Harper of course she is lost. It's almost ten o'clock at night and she is standing barefoot on a dark path going through the state park.

"I need you to take me home." She barely whispers and my heart goes cold. *Yeah, right crazy girl.*

"Okay, sure where is home?" *So your inbred brothers can murder me with banjos in the background.*

"It's 912 Maple Street." I try not to laugh out loud. That is the house next door to mine but no one has lived there in years. Its windows are boarded up. The grass is dead. We have lived next door for fourteen years and never once has anyone tried to visit it.

"Okay I live on Maple Street I can walk you that way." I am sure once we get on the street she will see her actual house. "Are you cold?" She is wearing the cutest jeans and a plain t-shirt but I am sure she needs something warmer.

"Nah, I am enjoying the cold weather." I start walking and she walks beside me. "I am hoping we get a real good snowfall this winter. I love going sledding in the park." It's March and the snow is just starting to melt but I won't comment on that. I am sure there isn't enough to get any real sledding done anymore.

"My little sister enjoys doing that with her friends. You may have seen them the past couple of months." I look down at her, and she glances up with a very serious look

"I doubt it. No one wants to play with me." She looks so sad I go to give her a side hug but she moves out of the way. She must not be a hugger. No big deal. We just continue on our way and I can't believe she isn't cold. I am trying not to shiver in my giant parka-like coat.

"I doubt that. You seem pretty cool!" I try to cheer her up but she doesn't even look up. I don't push the subject and just keep walking. I remember not believing my sister when she would tell me I was cool.

We walk for about fifteen minutes in complete silence before we get out of the park and under the actual street lights. I am excited to get out of the dark. I turn right, towards my house but as I do I realize that the little girl has stopped.

"Are you okay?" I don't even know her name. "I'm sorry, what's your name?"

She doesn't answer me. Her eyes are huge and she looks scared. "My momma is going to be so mad," she whispers. Ahh, she is out past curfew. I remember the worries of upsetting my mom. Heck, I still worry.

"No sweetie, your mom is probably worried." I stoop down to look into her eyes. "Let's get you home. They are probably out looking for you." She nods but stays in the shadows. I really hope her house is a safe place.

"Do you love your family?" She suddenly asks me.

"Of course, my parents are amazing. I have an older sister who is kind of flighty but while she forgot me today I love her. My little sister is crazy busy and drives me nuts trying to steal my makeup and uses my stuff without permission. Again though, I love her." Shrugging my shoulders I smile at the thought. "Do you have siblings?"

Looking down she kicks at the ground. "I did but momma sent them away."

Well, that is alarming. Again I wonder if she is safe. "Are you excited to go home?"

"No, but it's time." Okay, yeah. I am done. I stop fully and look at her.

"I can't take you to a place that you will be treated badly." Putting my hands on my hips like my mom does when lecturing us, I hope she takes me more seriously.

She just shrugs her shoulders and keeps walking. Wow, so this is how my mom feels when we ignore her. I am not impressed. I go to argue with her but then my name is shouted.

"Harper! Why are you out in the cold?!" I grin at my best friend in the whole world. Jagger makes his way over to me with a matching smile on his face. I notice he has cut his hair short on the sides again. I love this look on him. When we watch movies I often play with his hair and the short shaved sides are my favorite.

"Jag! I want you to meet…" I look down hoping maybe the little girl will say her name but she isn't there. "Ummm hello?" I call out turning around searching for any sign of my new friend. Moving closer to the bushes on the side of the sidewalk I start pushing leaves to the side. I hear Jagger walk up behind me.

"Umm Harper? What are you doing?" I am sure he is laughing as I am hip-deep in the Anderson's bushes, my ass in the air. I wonder if the little girl saw her house in the other direction? I stand up quickly and almost lose my balance. Jagger grabs my arms so I don't topple onto the ground. I swear I can feel the heat go through my coat and up my arms straight to my heart. Which is my biggest betrayer when it comes to Jagger. I am not supposed to be in love with my best friend. Yet, here I am. Trying not to drool while I look up into his dark blue eyes.

"T-tthannks." I stumble through the words and his eyebrows come down in a way that I know from years of being friends means he is concerned about me. "I was looking for the little girl walking with me. Did you see which way she went?" He looks up and glances around.

"No I didn't see a little girl with you." He pulls me a little closer without realizing what he is doing. He never notices how he makes me a priority. Most girls would be thrilled. Me? I hate that my best friend doesn't know how I truly feel.

His words finally sink through my lust filled head and I look around again. "She was right here with me. Maybe she went the other direction." I pick up my backpack where I had laid it next to the bushes and start to sling it back over my shoulder but Jagger effortlessly takes it from me. He just smirks when I glare at him and throws it over his shoulder. Holding out his other hand for me to take.

"Let's go look for your girl Harp." I smile at him. Of course he isn't going to let me go on my own. Just another reason I love this guy.

Chapter Two

"Where in the hell did she go?" I am practically shaking from the temperatures of the night. Jagger is practically holding me in his arms, walking behind me, to keep me warm. We have only been walking for about thirty minutes but a north wind came in and dropped the temperature by what feels like ten degrees.

"Maybe she found her house and went inside?" Jagger is now rubbing my arms trying to keep me from freezing. He knows I am a baby when it comes to the winter air in Colorado.

"Yeah maybe." I don't know where else she could be. We had turned around after about five blocks into searching in the opposite direction of our house for my mystery girl. Now we were almost home, I was happy to see the lights on in my living room and glanced over at Jagger's house. Since his mom died four years ago, no one would be up to wait for him. His older brother was working the night shift at the local lodge and his dad did graveyard for our local police department. My mom usually made extra food to put in their fridge every day.

Jagger's mom, Elizabeth, had been my mom's best friend. When the cancer came, it quickly took Elizabeth's life, it didn't just wreck one family but two. Mom has happily jumped in to help Albert, Jagger's dad, out with meals and helping with the boys. Jagger is a ski instructor at the resort during the winter and a physical therapist all year long. After my dad left the Marine Corps he moved us to Colorado. I was only five years old but I remember the first day I was playing in the yard when the cute dark-haired boy from next door asked if I wanted to see his fort in his backyard. Getting permission from my mom I spent the entire day making up a fictional world with Jagger and eating chocolate cookies until I wanted to get sick. We have been inseparable since. Fourteen years of friendship and about six years of being silently in love with him. I watched as he outgrew the awkward, zits, glasses, and braces age into the muscled hunk he is now. I watched the popular girls try to date him. Jagger never put up with them though seeing as most of them didn't understand that we were a package deal. I never really dated either. There hadn't ever been a guy who lived up to Jagger. I did have a couple friends thankfully. Friends that actually were in it for my friendship and not the chance of dating Jagger.

We have reached the end of my driveway and I start to break out of Jagger's arms. He turns me around, wrapping me into a big bear hug. He mumbles against my hair. I can't hear him but I don't want to pull away. He is bent at a weird angle and I am sure it hurts his back. I hate that I am only five foot five. I am such a shrimp compared to him. He pulls back.

"Did you hear me squirt?" Ugh, that nickname should have stayed in junior high. Rolling my eyes, I step back and shake my head no. Of course, I didn't hear him. I was too busy thinking about things I shouldn't be thinking about.

"I said you need to stop stressing out. I am sure your friend is fine and will show back up when you least expect it." I nod this time in agreement because I am sure he is right.

Jagger steps back and turns to cross the street to his house yelling over his shoulder, "See you tomorrow!"

I turn to go back into the house but a movement catches my attention. I turn fully towards the worn down two-story house next door. I squint to try to focus better but I can't make my feet move closer. Fear grips my heart. The curtain in the second story room is swishing back and forth. The scary part is. That is one of the only windows not boarded up or broken.

Backing away slowly until I get to my front steps and then I hurry to get inside. I remind myself that there is probably wind going through the house.

Chapter Three

I am so very tired of listening to Professor Lox discuss the need for more jobs in our small community to bring in more revenue. I took this business class to help dad with the books at his business. He is a private investigator. I am slightly jealous. I want to be the one who searches up and finds information on people. Sometimes for the good and sometimes for the bad. It truly doesn't bother me either way. I just have this drive to find things that aren't easy to find. My older sister, Layla, is almost ready to finish at the police academy. She wanted to be a bounty hunter after reading the Stephanie Plum novels growing up, but mom convinced her to go to the police academy. She is taking a few classes in criminal justice on the side. She says it's just 'in case', but I know it's because she really just wants to be a bounty hunter, and she kinda is.

"Harper Montgomery, why are you gracing me with your presence if it isn't to pay attention?" Professor Lox breaks me out of my internal debate about making a break out the back door so I don't fall asleep.

I hate being called out and my cheeks flame red when some of my classmates snicker. Acapella Lenord turns around throwing a red curl over her shoulder in a well-practiced move.

"She just doesn't want to let daddy down, Professor. Everyone knows Harper would rather be at the gym with all of the guys. You know, working up a sweat." She makes it sound like a sexual innuendo and I want to throat punch her but I just narrow my eyes. No bloodshed in public is my number one rule. I hate that she is one of those girls who is insecure and therefore hates that I hang out with Jagger and his friends.

"I am sorry Professor, I was just thinking I will need coffee this evening. It was a long day working at the gym. Leo was needing some," I pause acting like I can't find the right word, "help with his form." I smile at Acapella when I say this. She hates that I work with her boyfriend Leo but he has told her if she can't control her jealousy he will break up with her. 'No girl is worth that kind of trouble, no matter what they can do with their mouth,' is what he told me one time. I acted like I was throwing up because no matter how close we are I don't want to hear about him hooking up with the one person that has made it her personal mission to torture me all through high school. The only thing that could be worse is if it was Jagger hooking up with her.

The professor clears his throat and I look back at him with a fake smile on my face. Professor Lox is one of my favorite people in this town but I don't want to piss him off. Most don't know but he runs an underground business of spies, agents and others that will take care of any problem, for a price. The only reason I know this is because my best friends are his twin daughters, Max and Alex. They are also undercover spies and work with my father. They started to recruit me last year after seeing me spar with Jagger at the gym. My father and older sister were just as surprised as I was when I went to my first official meeting. Layla had been recruited two years prior and my dad was second in command of the organization. Dad had left the military but the military didn't leave him apparently. Now my dad runs the private investigator office. My mother loves that he has settled down so well after the Marines, thinking that being a P.I. is enough to quench dad's need for justice. Apparently, she doesn't know about his other job. It is probably for the best. Mom runs the bookshop and cafe with my aunt Marissa, her sister.

"Miss Montgomery, we are almost done for tonight. Why don't you head out a little early and grab some caffeine from the coffee cart." I try not to laugh at the fact that he doesn't say the name of the cart. "I heard they have a new special going today." I sit up straighter in my chair. I know he just gave me a code to go see Alex. Finally, I was going to get to go have some action.

"Yes sir, I am going to go do that right now." I throw everything into my backpack and practically trip over my feet getting out the door.

I rush out the doors of the B Building and out into the cold weather. I swear it's going to snow again. Colorado hates me. I take a left and see the small coffee stand with the umbrella parked over by the courtyard. There is the usual line. Alex and Max, along with their little sister Charlie, started their own business with one coffee stand on the campus by their dorm room and it had grown to have five stands all through the college campus in just the past year and a half. They named them to get back at their parents. One More Brewsky is a hint at the fact that each girl is named with the intention that most will think they are men. Their youngest sister is Nic as in Nicole, Maxie is

Max, Alexandria is Alex and Charlene is Charlie. So while the name of the coffee stands suggests there is alcohol being served, they are just a coffee stand.

I step in line and start looking through my notifications on my phone. My sister wrote me to say she would once again not be picking me up and that I should write Jagger for a ride as tonight was my late night. A message from Jagger shows that won't be an option as he is going to stay at Leo's place. They plan on eating pizza and trash-talking to little kids while playing Fortnite. This means there is no way he will remember to come pick me up. Sending him a quick text telling him to not make any kids cry tonight, I stick my phone in my back pocket. I am almost to the front of the line and Alex sends me a wink over the head of the customer in front of me. The customer turns to look at me, giving me the stank eye. Of course, it's Jeffery Lenord, Acapella's brother. I swear their family doesn't know how to be nice. Jeffery has never done anything like Acapella but he also never smiles at me and doesn't stop his sister when she starts fights with me or others.

"Hi Jeffery, I just left your sister in class. A delight as always." I fake a smile again. I know I am starting shit with a man who is easily six five and around two hundred and fifty pounds. I just don't care. His eyebrows actually go down in a deeper frown than usual. I didn't know it was possible. He turns away from me without a word, grabs his coffee and then does something I didn't know was possible. He smiles at my best friend before heading off into the direction I just came from. My mouth hangs open in shock and I get jostled from behind as a reminder to keep the line moving. I go forward with my order but I am still rendered speechless so Alex just laughs and starts my coffee.

"Close your mouth Harper you are going to catch flies." Alex throws over her shoulder as she works with the complicated coffee maker. I watch her hands move swiftly and can't help but be a little jealous. Alex and Max have always moved with such grace. I however move like a fighter. Which in a way, I am. I fell in love with MMA fighting when my uncle Sutton, Marissa's husband, was babysitting me. Sutton owns the only gym with a sparring ring within a one hundred mile radius. He saw the love in my eyes and instantly talked to my dad into letting me fight. My mom was not impressed at first so my uncle made her come watch me practice. Suzanne Montgomery is alot of things but stupid is not one of them. She tells me all the time that it took one time watching me and she knew I found my niche. I love that she supports me and of course my dad was all for it.

Finally, I remember the real reason I am here. "Your dad sent me?"

"Yeah, but we will talk tomorrow morning." Alex hands me my coffee, refuses my money and sends me on my way. Damn, I love her.

Chapter Four

These classes took way too long. I can't believe I didn't fall asleep, especially in my math class. I hate how math is taught. I struggle with understanding the way the teacher wants my answers explained. I don't know how to explain my answer, I just got this number. Jagger's brother, Ezra, spent hours with a giant whiteboard trying to help me but after almost three days of torture he gave up.

Before I step outside I wrap my scarf around my neck up to my nose. The windows showed the snow starting to fall. I can't believe I forgot to ask Alex for a damn ride.

I walk out into the big fluffy flakes falling from the sky and start off towards the park. I had stayed a few minutes late to find something in the library and the college seems pretty dead now. My mind wanders off thinking about Jagger. I don't know how to get over him. I really want to go off and fall in love, get married and have kids. Kinda hard when the man who is perfect for me is next door, my best friend and thinks of me as one of the guys. Sometimes I picture just walking up and kissing him. Like one of those surprise reaction videos. I picture him telling me, he's always been in love with me but didn't want to lose our friendship. However, I know he won't do that. I am so lost in thought I almost run right into the little girl again.

"Holy shit balls!" I grasp at my chest like my great aunt Betsy whenever someone starts to get to kinky on the TV. You'd think she had never had sex before. Six kids prove that is a lie. "You scared me!" She is wearing the same clothes as before but this time her hair is in a ponytail. "Why are you out so late again?" She smiles and steps closer to me.

"I wasn't sure I'd see you again." She tilts her head to the side. Looking me up and down. "I missed you the past couple of days." She smiles then turns around to start walking towards my house.

"Where did you go the other night? I wanted you to meet my best friend Jagger. He would have walked you home with me." I smile and walk beside her. Suddenly I remembered something, "Hey what's your name?"

"I don't remember my name." She whispers to me.

"What do you mean, sweetie? What does your mom call you?" I stop and so does she. It suddenly dawns on me. "Are you not supposed to tell strangers your name?"

"No, I just don't remember it. My momma just calls me Kid. I don't like it but I answer because if I don't she won't…" Her eyes get wide once she realizes that she has said too much.

"Are you excited for the snow Harper?" She changes the subject and I let her because I know better than to push a pre-teen about something they don't want to talk about. Everly, my youngest sister, had just turned thirteen and is tight-lipped about everything lately. It kills my mom because she thinks Layla and I told her everything. She would be so upset if she knew I harbored a huge crush on Jagger and never told her.

"I am not, honestly. Jagger, the best friend I mentioned earlier, is a ski instructor and will probably drag me out to the mountain this weekend if the snow keeps falling." I don't mind skiing however I do mind that I have to share Jagger with all the snow bunnies that follow him around. I know that Max and Alex will be there thankfully. "Are you excited about the snow?" I know she is the way she keeps hopping around and trying to catch snowflakes in her mouth. I can't believe she isn't shivering in her threadbare shirt. I have seen Leo, Jagger and the other guys play basketball shirtless in the snow so I guess I shouldn't be surprised at others' ability to handle the cold weather versus mine.

"I really am. My mom doesn't like the snow but she likes that I am not in the house bothering her." Now my heart is breaking for this sweet girl. I want to hug her but I remember what happened the last time.

"What did you do today?" My turn to change the subject. I don't want to push her about this horrible mother of hers.

"I am not allowed out during the day. I have to stay inside where others won't see me. Momma says that I will scare people. You are actually the first person I have talked to in a while." She isn't paying attention to me so I am sure she missed the look on my face. You know the one where I contemplate murder of the mother of this sweet girl.

"Do you know your momma's name?" Oh yeah, I am getting this girl out of her house no matter what. This question catches the sweet girl off guard because she stops and glances at me.

"Why do you want my mom's name? If you tell her

about us being friends, she will make me leave." She looks like she is going to cry and I can't have that.

"Never mind. I was going to see if she would let you come to our house to hang out sometime." I keep walking and notice we are almost at the turn for my street. I turn right just like last time and I notice that my friend stays close to the shadows again. I don't mention it and soon we are getting close to my house. "Honey, you got to tell me where you live so I can take you home. This is my house right here." I point at our two-story ranch style home.

"I know." She quickly rushes past me and goes between my house and the house next door. "I see you hang out all the time." She says this as she disappears into the yard of 912 Maple Street. The one that is completely vacant. Isn't it?

Chapter Five

Whoever said that sisters are a girl's best friend did not have a scaredy-cat Layla as their older sister. After the little girl went between the houses I ran inside the house and tried to beg Layla into going next door and searching to see if there are squatters. This big bad wanna-be bounty hunter told me no.

"Hell no Harper. That house is scary as hell. I park my car on the other side of the house just so I don't have to walk by there at night." Layla is completely snuggled in her covers. Her raven black hair is up in a messy bun that only models and Layla can pull off. She is reading Rule by L.A.-Cotton, one of her favorite indie authors.

"Come on Layla. That little girl is scared out of her mind. I could tell her momma must hurt her or something." I bat my eyes and try to look innocent and pleading. She doesn't give though. I leave and go straight into my room. I throw my backpack on my bed and start for the closet only to notice my window shade is open. I hate having my window open as it faces the worn-down house. I can't help but look over there now and scream.

There in the window across from mine is a rather large woman. She is wearing a smock and her gray hair is up in a bun. She is staring straight at me and I can't help but fall to the ground. Like somehow that will make it so she can't see me. I army crawl to the wall and pull myself up slowly to look over the window sill. She is still there but this time she looks even more pissed off. She raises one hand and acts like she is cutting her throat with her finger. I quickly close the curtains and run back into Layla's room.

Throwing open the door I practically dive onto Layla who tries to get out of the way,

"What the hell Harper!" She shoves at me but I am not moving.

"She freaking saw me, Lay!" I whisper to her. "The mom was looking right into my room and she threatened me!"

"Okay, okay calm down. How did she threaten you?" She gets up, leaving me in her bed, and goes to her closet grabbing a sweatshirt that looks vaguely familiar. Is that Ezras? I will have to ask her about it when I am not scared that some lady is going to come kill me and my family in my sleep. Just as her head pops through the sweatshirt her bedroom door slams open. I will not even lie, we both screamed. Layla somehow ends up back in her bed and we are both hiding under her cover.

"What in the hell are you two going off about?!" My father bellows. I sometimes forget that he was in the Marines so long. Then he uses his cadence voice and we all pay attention. I have seen grown men piss themselves when dad is angry.

"Dad the lady next door just threatened to kill me!" I throw myself at him. I can take a lot but apparently not today. "I think she is hurting her daughter and when I.."

"Wait. Wait, you are saying Mrs. Gilch just threatened

to kill you?" He pulls me back to look me in the eye. He sounds like he doesn't believe me and I don't blame him. Mrs. Gilch is the sweetest woman you will ever meet. She is ninety and lives with her four shih tzu-terrier mixes and I have no idea the number of cats. However she is not the neighbor I am worried about.

"No dad, I think there are squatters at 912!" He lets me go and turns towards the door.

"Alright, let's go check this shit out." No one said Brant Montgomery wasn't a badass. He totally is. I follow him out with Layla on my heels. Apparently, she isn't so scared when dad is with us. We stop long enough to grab our shoes and my coat at the bottom of the stairs. Dad runs to the kitchen and grabs the extra flashlights. And I make sure I have my cell phone in case we need to call 911.

Stepping out of the house and heading straight over to the abandoned house I notice the front door is boarded pretty well. I glance up at the window, where I had seen the moving curtain the other night and I see the little girl staring down at me. She looks so sad. I know she thinks that her mom will make her go away but my dad will stop that. I wave at her. I watch as a tear slips down her face and she turns away from the window.

"Harper over here!" My dad's yell brings me back to what we are doing and I notice him and Layla have gone around the house looking for ways to enter. I quickly reach them in time to see dad shimmy one of the boards off the side door.

"Ladies first." Dad steps back and gestures to Layla and I. Layla steps back and gives me the nod to go first. Of course, she isn't going first. I step over the bottom board and duck under the top board that is still covering the doorway. Nothing but darkness meets me.

Chapter Six

"Harper, move out of the way so I can get in." My sister pushes her hand through pushing on my butt. It's enough to jolt me out of my fear of the dark enough that I remember to turn on my flashlight. I swear this is like walking into a bad Supernatural show. Okay with Dean and Sam there are no "bad" shows. Layla steps up next to me and turns on her flashlight. Dad easily maneuvers his large frame through the door and steps in front of us to lead the way. I take the rear so that Layla doesn't freak at every creak of the old house. She raises her eyebrow at me and I smile.

"This way if someone comes from behind you can still run to safety as they take me somewhere to murder me." She rolls her eyes at my statement but dad laughs. He knows she was worried about that exact thing. We had entered what looked like a mudroom of a sort and dad quickly moves to the hallway. Taking a left he checks the few open doors. Nothing but cobwebs and some broken furniture. At the end of the hallway is the back of the house and an open kitchen. To the right is a stairway that leads up. A door next to the stairs hangs on its hinges and it leads downstairs.

"I really hope that isn't where you want to start dad." I whisper and he shakes his head.

"Where did she threaten you from?" He whispers back to me.

"The room across from mine." He nods that he hears me then slowly makes his way up the stairs. Layla's flashlight reflects off his hunting knife that's strapped to his belt. I love that he is always prepared. The woman upstairs scares the crap outta me. I follow Layla trying to step where she has stepped to make sure we don't hit any creaky floor boards. Dad gets to the top and leans back then quickly jumps out in case someone is at the top of the stairs ready to fight him. No one is and we start down the long hallway. Looking in all the doorways to the right and left. Again more empty rooms. In fact, it doesn't even seem like anyone has been squatting.

As my dad reaches the room that would be across from mine he pauses at the closed door. He looks back at me with his eyebrow raised in question. I nod once to answer his unspoken question. He wants to make sure this is the right room. I know he doesn't make mistakes, he just wants me to feel a part of this.

He opens the door slowly and the door creaks open. I am a little shocked that there is an actually functional door. Nothing else in the house seemed to be. Layla follows around the corner and her small gasp hits me before I make it into the room. I come inside and come to a full stop. The room is lit up with candles. Kids' toys are all over and there is a little bed in the corner. Pretty pink bedspread and pillows decorate the bed.

The door slams shut behind me and I turn quickly. There is no one there and when I grab the knob to get out it seems to be jammed. I look over at my dad who is carefully looking through the stuff.

"The door is locked." I tell him and he squats down to pick up a doll that is sitting at a small table with a tea set.

"Harper, come here." I walk over to him. My heart is beating in my chest at the complete calmness of my dad's voice. He never is this calm unless it's bad news. Dad stands fully as I make my way over to him. Layla is on his other side but she is looking at the dolls that are still around the table.

I look at the doll in my dad's hands. I suddenly can't swallow. It's me. A perfect replica of me the first day I met the little girl.

"What is going on?" I ask my dad. I am completely confused. Have they been following me?

"Harper, look at these." I look down and want to throw up. There in a perfect circle at the table having a small tea party are dolls that look like all my friends. Layla, Max, Alex, Charlie and even Everly and Nic. The one that makes my blood go completely cold is the one of Jagger. He is wearing his favorite hoodie and basketball shorts. His dark hair is perfectly styled, just the way I like it. His eyes though, his eyes are covered in black X's.

"What the hell is going on here?" I ask the room in general.

"We need to call the police now." My father says and I grab my phone and make the call. We take photos of the room for our own files. It doesn't take long for the police to arrive and come upstairs. The door is still locked but they find the old skeleton key on the floor by the door.

There are no shoe prints throughout the house that don't belong to my family or I. The police take in all the dolls as evidence. While they are doing their job I send out a mass text to make sure everyone is okay. I am not really surprised the only person I don't hear back from instantly is Jagger. I knew he was at Leo's place hanging out. However, as the police are getting done with our statements I get a message from Jagger saying he is coming home to see me and make sure I am alright.

I love that he wouldn't take no for an answer but him doing things like this isn't helping my heart not fall deeper in love.

"Alright girls let's go." My dad holds out his arm for me to come to him but I remember that this window looks directly into my room. I move over to close the shade and stop in my tracks. There on the window in sloppy cursive etched in the frost is a note to me. I am positive it wasn't there before.

Harper,
I just wanted to be friends.
Help Me

I had never given my little friend my name.

Acknowledgments and Thank Yous

Huge shout out to the other ladies in this anthology for putting up with my questions and learning process.
Kassie and Jenee. I have no words to describe what you two mean to me. Thank you for letting me be part of your world.
Ebonie, for going through this book, talking me off my ledges and cheering me on in life.
Holley, for telling me to stop doubting myself.
My kids, for letting me shut you out of my office and giving me names for characters when I was at a loss! You guys are rockstars!
My Grandma Leta, for always believing in me.

Necro: A Rejected Mates Prequel

BY: ALEXIS TAYLOR

Ghost Level

To all the supernatural creatures out there. If you want to hang out with a geeky human I totally volunteer.

P.S. sorry if I got anything wrong, don't kill me. I will learn for next time. Love your willing victim Alexis xoxo

P.P.S If you're a hot vampire, werewolf, gargoyle oh hell if you're hot anything I am totally single and don't judge.

Chapter One

At seventeen years old you would think my life would be pretty easy right? School, homework, deciding what to do after graduation. But no; my life was anything but. Seeing as, since I was five I had been able to see and communicate with the dead. If that wasn't bad enough I could even sense supernaturals. It had been quite a shock the first time I had pointed out a vampire. Just a lovely trait that my absentee father had passed down to me before he abandoned me. Before I was adopted, all of the foster families and my caseworker had thought I was crazy. They would see me talking to myself, hanging out in graveyards, and researching things no normal child would. Not only that, but I talked about the supernaturals that I saw. Wanting to learn more about them. Wanting to know if I was the only one who could see them. Moving around a lot helped. Most kids thought I was insane, others just thought that I was dangerous. It didn't leave much room for friendships, especially once I had hit my teenage years. Kids could be cruel but teenagers were almost as evil as the spirits I attracted. I soon learned to hide what I could do. I even stopped talking to the other kids and the teachers unless I absolutely had to.

It had made for a very lonely childhood, thankfully though I had my Nona. My adoptive dad's mother was a little eccentric but never doubted anything I told her. Whenever a spirit was difficult or vengeful, which was always, she helped me any way she could, finding ways to help me protect myself, and whoever the spirit was haunting. She would never tell me how though. Any time I asked she would say now wasn't the time and while she was here, it was something I wouldn't have to worry about. She would always protect me until her dying day.

Over the years we had encountered some truly evil spirits but helping the living even if they would never know made me feel like I had a purpose. That maybe I wasn't just another unwanted kid.

Being able to see the dead didn't help me as much as I had hoped. I couldn't prevent my adoptive parents from being killed a few months ago. Thankfully, Nona had fought to have me come live with her. She at least didn't blame me for failing to protect her son and his wife. That only made me more determined to find the spirit who hurt them. I had high hopes that the move to Nona's would help me pull myself out of the guilt hole that I had fallen in. Even though I knew I wasn't at fault, that didn't stop the crippling depression that threatened to overwhelm me.

For most the thought of moving to another new town, and starting another new school would have been insane, but I couldn't wait. I needed a fresh start to escape the whispers and accusations from the close-minded people in this town. Being unknown would give me the time and space I would need to find and finally avenge the spirits who turned my life upside down.

I knew it would end up being more of the same. Crazy Kat, always talking to herself. That was what they said around here. Even though I was more than a little apprehensive. I knew that at least for the first little bit, I could pretend to be normal. At the very least, have some friends for a few weeks before they dipped out at the fact that I was weird.

All the places that I had lived before were huge compared to the town Nona lived in. It was slightly daunting. However, secretly I was beyond excited by how small the town of Inferie Springs was. Hopefully, they wouldn't have a huge supernatural presence and I could maybe finally have a normal life.

"Kat, Honey we're here. Go grab your bag and I will get dinner started. We need to have a talk before you rest." Nona's voice snapped me out of my thoughts. I hadn't realized the car had even stopped.

I didn't even have a chance to get out of the car before I felt it. The haze that came over me when a supernatural was here. Seriously, they couldn't have at least waited until I settled in. Given me a small chance to pretend that I was a normal teen.

Normally, I couldn't sense what kind of Supe it was. The weight on my chest intensified as it got closer, signifying that it was in fact a Supe. Ghosts made me nauseous, Supes had me feeling like I had ten pounds of something sitting on my chest. I had two choices though, I could pretend not to notice and hope they couldn't tell what I was or I could go ahead and take care of it. Either way, I had a feeling that I was going to be hurting later. Supes weren't always the nicest of people.

Looking back quickly, I saw that Nona had made it into the house. Thank God, that was one less thing that I had to worry about. Now I just had to worry about myself, but the

Supe took that choice away from me as he sped so close that he was a blur.

I had to suck in a breath forcing the air out of my lungs and back in as the weights intensified. Fuck, this was not how this should have gone.

"Well, hello there little one." He said, his ruby red lips moving to reveal fangs and instant fear hit me.

I didn't even hear the sound of the door open, but Nona's voice filled the air before the Vampire got any closer.

"Fred, I told you to give me a little time. She doesn't know yet." She yelled as my head whipped towards her. Fred? What the hell it seemed that she was friendly with him.

"I am so sorry Mable, I couldn't resist. I could smell her all the way across town. Don't you think it's about time you introduced me to my granddaughter?" He shot back causing me to turn back to him.

"You both better come on inside. It looks like we all need to have a talk." She replied with one last look before going into the house. Fred speeding over to her to follow behind, leaving me out here with more questions than I could even count.

So much for that normal teenage life that I wanted. "Wait, what do you mean granddaughter!!!!"

Chapter Two

LUKE

"I am sorry, there is nothing more that we can do. We have run every test and done everything that we can to help you." The doctor in front of me said. I had known that it was pointless, but it was a town of supernaturals so if anyone could have found what was wrong. It would have been him.

"So what does that mean?" I asked, already knowing what he was going to tell me. Whatever I had going on was eating away at me, slowly taking everything from me. My health, my looks, hell probably even my soul.

"It means that we can send you home with meds that will keep you comfortable, but unfortunately unless you wish to use a more supernatural form of medicine. There's nothing else I can offer you." He said, giving me the answer that I had already known.

"What exactly are you trying to tell me?" I wanted him to lay it all out for me so that maybe it would help take my choice away. Jake and Cass had been offering to turn me since my health had started to flag, but I had always stayed so sure that something would help.

"What I mean is, you have friends in the supernatural community. If you let any of them turn you, then you would have their immune system and I have never known a human illness that could outlast that." He replied saying just as I knew that he would. They were right, I was going to die or change to something other than a human.

"Thank you for seeing me." That was all I could muster to say as the Doctor looked at me with pity. I had known this would be the outcome.

Grabbing my jacket, I headed out of the exam room. I knew the guys would be waiting outside the hospital and I went as slow as I could. This wasn't something that I wanted to talk about, but I had no choice. I was dying, there was no beating around the bush. This was going to suck.

After stalling as long as I could, I opened the main doors of the hospital and headed out. Just as I had expected, all four of them were standing against a tree in sight of the door. The downside of going to the only Supernatural doctor in the town was that I now had to go tell them what he said. I had to tell my best friends I was dying and there was nothing we could do. Unless I asked one of them to turn me, which I knew Ash and Klaus were dead set against. They had made it very clear, I was to stay human.

"It's bad, right? I can smell the fear and worry from here. They can't help you?" Cass was in front of me before I could nod. His arms pulled me in for the quickest hug I had ever got.

I couldn't help but laugh at his face. My manly badass werewolf best friend showing any sort of emotion was rare. Cass willingly touching another person was something that never happened. Not unless it was with his fist.

"God, Cass I need to be dying before you hug me. I'm

hurt, man, seriously." I knew I was deflecting what I had to say with my usual humor but I honestly didn't know how to tell them. Hell, I didn't even want to accept it myself.

You don't have to tell them. Luke, I already know. Do you want to go home? I can fill them in if you need time to yourself. Jake's voice filled my mind and the relief I felt slammed into me over his words. Even if I was a little annoyed he had read my mind again.

I knew that we needed to talk about it, but right now I was having a hard enough time just standing here. It was time for me to lay down and rest. As usual, my energy didn't last long.

"Okay guys, Luke is going home to rest. We will leave him to do this and we can talk when he is ready. Do you want one of us to take you home?" Jake said leaving no room for arguments. He had a way of making the authority clear in his voice. Maybe it was a vamp thing, it usually irritated me, but today I was so glad for it I could have cried.

"Thanks, man I could have taken care of it though and I will just grab an uber," I replied, he knew how thankful I was for what he said. It didn't need to be said out loud again. Just because I was sick didn't mean I didn't need to be coddled.

When you are ready, we can talk and discuss our options. Now take your ass home. Jake's voice floated into my head again, and I just nodded before pulling up the uber app. A car would be here in just a few minutes and then I could go take a nap.

"Will you stop having secret conversations with him and let him go. Damn it, Jake! You don't have to control every little thing he does." With a nod of his head, Cass took off. Silently heading towards the woods, no doubt to shift and run until he exhausted himself. That's what he always did when there was an issue with one of us he couldn't fix.

Thankfully, my uber got here before any of the others could start their usual theatrics. Watching them fade away as I got further away, I was so grateful that I had them.

As we passed the school, I knew I would need to prepare. If I was going to turn into something, I needed to keep my grades up and for that, I needed to rest. I could already tell this year was going to suck. But if it meant staying alive, I would do whatever it takes.

Chapter Three

KAT

My Grandfather was a vampire. Honestly out of everything they had just told me, that part was what I was struggling with most. As a vampire, he should have been able to save my parents, why didn't he? Why didn't they tell me that they were truly family, not strangers who felt bad for the abandoned kid? But family. My birth Dad, Michale, had taken off with me just days after mom had died. Running from Nona and his brother, the only other family we had in hope that I wouldn't have the gift. As if distancing us from them would stop what was inevitably going to come. When it was obvious that I could communicate with the dead, he left me outside a church and took off. No one had heard from him since.

Somehow knowing my aunt and uncle wanted me and had spent years tracking me down made things a little easier to deal with. It eased a part of myself that I hadn't even realized needed soothing. Then again, I thought that all adopted kids felt that unwanted feeling in the pit of their bones. However, what I was having a hard time with was the fact that they had hidden what Nona was. That I had a grandfather. That I had a family. How had they been so easily killed if they were part of the supernatural world? I had so many questions but I just couldn't ask. Not right now. I needed time to get my thoughts to myself.

"Can I go to my room? I know we have a lot to talk about and I have a lot of questions but I just need some time to think first. If that's ok?" Nona looked at me with sadness in her eyes before nodding. I knew that she was taking this as a dismissal and it wasn't, but I just needed to get away.

"Your room is on the second floor. The whole floor is yours. We wanted to give you some space to yourself. Go rest. I will call you when dinner is ready. I left some things you'll need for school tomorrow on your bed." I couldn't look at either of them as I silently headed to my room.

Ugh, school? How had I forgotten about that? I made my way up the stairs and found my room easily. It was the bright purple one that stood out. Purple had always been my favorite color. It was beautiful and I couldn't wait to see the inside. Shutting the door behind me, I closed my eyes leaning on the door.

Everything will be okay Kat they love you and want you here. Even if one of them is a Vampire, you've dealt with worse. I thought a few times hoping that it would actually sink in. Shaking my head, I finally opened my eyes to find my adoptive dad, or well I guess now I should call him Uncle Max, standing before me with a huge smile on his blood-covered face. Before I could scream, his ice-cold hand covered my face.

"Kitty Kat, I need you to not scream and just listen to me, ok? I know this is a lot to take in but I'm here to help you. I am going to remove my hand but I need you to promise me you will stay calm and listen. Okay, sweetie?" I had seen a lot of ghosts in my life but never anyone I had known. Never anyone I had loved and very rarely was the ghost nice. They were usually angry and determined to inflict as much horror and pain as possible.

Nodding my head, he removed his hand from my mouth and looked at me as if he was waiting for me to speak. However, I was struck speechless. I had no words for the torrent of emotions that flooded me at the sight of him. His eyes were filled with pain as he finally spoke.

"I couldn't leave you. Not when there was so much I didn't get a chance to tell you before we died. So I didn't cross over with your aunt. I chose to stay here and guide you for as long as I can. Now I know you have questions so I will answer as much as I can." He said, his voice filling me with a calm that I hadn't felt since he had died. Other than the bloody cut on his head, he looked like himself.

"You couldn't leave me? But you did, you have been gone for months. Why didn't you come back sooner?" The words were ripped from my soul before I could stop myself. I heaved a huge sob as the tears slammed into me and my heart felt as though it was going to explode.

"Oh, Hunny. I didn't want to leave you. We had planned to tell you everything that night. I don't really remember what happened when we died but I knew I wasn't ready to move on. Your aunt wanted to go be with her parents. But me, I wanted to be here and be with our girl until she was ready for me to go. I am so sorry I wasn't here sooner baby. You know that you are my everything." The pain in my heart lessened as I looked up back into his eyes. He had chosen to stay on earth with me. Rather than be with his wife, he stayed to help me. I couldn't be angry at him after hearing that. I could only feel pain and guilt... they had both put me first since I had come to live with them. And now I was the reason they were apart.

"Are you sure?" I asked through a sob even though I

knew I shouldn't have. What I should have done was made him move on, or sent him away, but I couldn't. I needed help, and I needed him. He was the only dad I had ever known.

"Of course I am. Now, you have a big day ahead of you tomorrow. This town is like nothing you have ever known and if anyone can help find answers about you it is the people here. We will work through this together and I will stay as long as you need me." He said as I looked him over again. I was half scared to look away for fear that he would disappear and be gone for good.

"Do you promise?" my voice quivered as I asked and I wanted to wince. Why could I not get my emotions under control?

"I do, and we have plenty of time to talk. I can see how exhausted you are and how much you already have to think over. Get some rest and we can talk after school tomorrow. I am so proud of you Kitty Kat." He said with a smile and a kiss to the forehead before blinking out and leaving me alone. Tears still fell from my eyes before I wiped them away.

I needed to shower, but I was beyond exhausted. I would just have to do it in the morning. Wasting no time, I grabbed the bag with my pajamas in it and changed before face-planting on the queen-sized sleigh bed. Tomorrow I would think more about all the information that had been slammed into my head. My last thought before I floated into unconsciousness was that there was a possibility that here I could be myself and still be accepted.

Chapter Four

"Goodmorning dear, I made you some eggs and toast just like you like it," Nona said as I walked into the kitchen. The look on her face made my heart hurt, but I wasn't ready to one-hundred percent forgive her yet. She may not have bold faced lied to me, but she had omitted a hell of a lot and it hurt.

"Thank you, Nona," I replied stiffly and grabbed the plate on the counter that had been laid out for me. I could feel her staring at me as I ate, it was as if her eyes were boring holes into the back of my neck

"You remember where the school is? I showed it to you on the way." Nona asked and I just nodded my head unsure of where this was going. "Well, I was saving this for your birthday, but I figured you wouldn't want your Nona driving you to school your senior year." She continued with a huge smile on her face while throwing a set of keys on the counter.

"Nona, what?" was all I was able to get out as the shock of what she said hit me. I had never owned a vehicle before.

"With everything that is going on, I know that you aren't happy with me. However, trust me when I say that I didn't tell you just to not tell you. You will figure it out on your eighteenth birthday and I wish on everything in this world that I could tell you. I love you so much, Kitty Kat." Her sad eyes pulled at my heart and I knew that even though I was angry I couldn't stay mad at her. She had always been my constant.

"I understand, I'm not happy about it, but I forgive you. I love you too Nona and I will see you after school." I replied as I pulled her to me and wrapped my arms around her. She was home to me.

"Get on out of here then. Don't be doing any of those burnouts all the other kids do." She laughed as I grabbed my bag and headed out to see a gorgeous truck waiting for me.

It was a midnight blue with silver accents and I was instantly enamored. I ran my hand along the side as I opened the driver's door and climbed in. This was more than I ever expected or could have imagined.

Chapter Five

CASS

Irritation flowed through me as yet another female in our pack strutted her way by me in the hallway. Couldn't they see that I wasn't interested right now, it was obvious that my only interest now was Luke. I watched as he tried to contain his limp and failed. He would have a fit if I went over to help him walk, my wolf was riding me to go help. Sometimes it was hard to ignore my nature, I just barely managed.

"How are you doing today, man?" I said as he came to his locker which was conveniently beside mine. We had made sure that he would be with one of us at all times and I had hallway duty.

"I feel like run over shit. That was a stupid question." He replied with a smirk where the humor didn't reach his eyes. His whole face was drawn in pain and it broke me.

"You will be okay," I knew I said that more to myself than to him, but it had to be the truth. He was my brother, it didn't matter that we shared blood and if it came down to it I would turn him. Whether he wanted me to or not.

Klaus was standing at the doorway and nodded his

head in signal that he would take over Luke watch, which was good because I had to get to homeroom, which was across the damn school. I could act upset about it all I wanted, but usually, I enjoyed the walk. It was nice to be left alone at least for a minute. Being the Alpha's son had awarded me pretty much famous status in town and while I liked the ladies it sent my way, I hated everything else.

The whole school was abuzz though and for once it wasn't about me or the guys. Apparently, we were getting a new girl, which hardly ever happened. So everyone in the school was already gossiping about her. It seemed like no one knew anything which resulted in the masses making outlandish assumptions. I couldn't honestly give a shit about that though, I didn't have time for anything but a quick lay and even those were losing their appeal.

Paying the whispers no mind, I continued on hoping that she would continue to give the people something to talk about. Then they would at least quit whispering about what I was doing. It got old fast.

Turning a corner, I slammed into someone and my world stopped. My wolf came to life as I felt a searing pain in my chest and I knew that I had just gotten my mate mark. A small strawberry blonde girl was in front of me. Her green eyes, which looked a little too big for her face but somehow worked, stared me down.

"Sorry about that, I was trying to find a classroom." Ahh, the new girl I thought as I took a breath and everything was instantly ruined. The underlying scent of Myrrh told me that a necromancer was in front of me and she was my mate. "What is going on?"

I shoved back and growled as my wolf begged me to get closer, but that could never happen. Not after one of her kind had killed my mother. Mate or no, I could just strangle her for what she was alone. I had half a mind to do just that.

"This will never happen. Mates or no, I would never want to be around a necromancer. Why don't you crawl back to whatever hole you crawled out of?" I growled as I fought to take my eyes off her. Why would the fates do this to me?

"Mates? Necromancer? Excuse the fuck out of me, but I was just trying to find my homeroom. You will not talk to me that way!" She yelled, her voice getting louder as I saw a second of hurt in her eyes. I didn't give a fuck if I hurt her, and I was going to prove it right now.

Stepping in close, her breath held as she looked up into my eyes. There was a fire there and I had one second to wish that she had been any other supernatural. However, her scent hit my nose again and this time I did growl.

"I don't give a fuck what you were trying to do or where you are going. I reject any thoughts of you being my mate. You best avoid me from now on because I will make your life hell. No one here will accept you. Hope you like to be alone," I replied not even trying to keep my hatred out of my voice.

"I just want to find my class." Her voice was even as she spoke and I knew that she wanted to say more, but I could sense her fear and see the sprinkling of tears in her eyes. At least she was smart enough to know not to pop off.

"And I said I don't give a fuck. I run this school and you will stay out of my way or I will make sure you don't come back." It was an empty threat, but she didn't have to know that. I popped out my chest and it slammed into her small frame, causing her to fall to the floor. "You just don't know what you have gotten yourself into here, little girl."

I didn't wait to see if she would get up or how she would respond. I just walked by her and continued to Ms.

Callens' homeroom. No one here would accept her, I hadn't lied about that. Necros were the lowest of the low. All that had been documented were evil and I believed it seeing as one had killed my mother when I was only six.

There would be more hell to pay once my father found out about this. I wouldn't be surprised if he found some way to kill the girl. A thought that had my heart clench until I shoved it down. My wolf fought against me, he wanted her but he knew it was for the best, or he would over time. Mate mark or not, I would never stoop so low.

Chapter Six

KAT

I sat on the floor for a few seconds unable to process what just happened or why my heart was aching the way it was. The boy, who I could only guess was a shifter, had all but attacked me and yet all I wanted to do was be near him. What the fuck was wrong with me? It didn't matter though he could take whatever just happened and shove it up his ass.

After a few more seconds of thought, I shook it off. I had dealt with plenty of bullies before and it wouldn't stop me. Someone here had to be okay with the fact that I was, as he said, a Necro. Not that I was a hundred percent sure what exactly that meant. However, I got the feeling that it wasn't a good thing. Nevertheless, I would ask my Uncle about it.

Finally, after what felt like forever, I found the class just as the bell for homeroom rang and I was a little glad I had managed to avoid that asshole. I had hoped for a normal school day and for the most part I got it. At least until the last class of the day when my uncle popped in and refused to leave. His running commentary was starting to get hard to ignore.

"Oh man, if she had been a teacher back in my day I would have paid better attention when I was your age." He said as I shot him a look because there was no way I could talk back without everyone in this class hearing me. However, that didn't stop me from pulling out a piece of paper and writing back.

I am trying to not draw attention to myself. What are you doing here? I wrote on my paper before giving him a pointed look which he thankfully got.

"Well, I know how bad first days can be and I wanted to just check-in and see how things were going." He said and as much as I loved that he was here to check on me. I knew there was another reason as well.

Did you know that I would have issues here because of what I am? What is a Necro? Does mate mean what I think it does? There are so many things we need to talk about. Meet me in the parking lot after school and you can ride home with me and we can talk.

"Where did you hear those words? I had hoped that you wouldn't have issues because of what you are, but unfortunately, Necromancers don't have a good name. Mates mean exactly what you think, when you get done for the day we have to have a long chat and I swear to fill you in on everything." He replied before disappearing to wherever ghosts went when they couldn't be seen.

My thoughts were in an uproar as I thought over his words. I had really hoped to fit in here, but that seemed like more of a pipe dream judging by the stares and the shifter's reaction to me. Just thinking of him made my heart clench, and that instantly pissed me off. He didn't want to be mates with me because of something as stupid as what I was. Yeah, I didn't know a lot, but I knew enough that I had half a mind to find him and give him a piece of it. Fucking ass!

The final bell rang and I couldn't get out of my seat fast enough. I wasn't scared by any means, but my heart had been throbbing all day. I was pissed all I wanted was to take off, drive in my baby, and get answers from my uncle.

He must have felt me thinking of him or something because as soon as I stepped out of the school doors there he was. Standing there as he would if he had been there to pick me up. A cut of sadness slammed me, but I canned it because at least he was here. He fell into step beside me.

I was almost home free in the parking lot when I was struck by that feeling. The feeling of overwhelming despair, my stomach rolled and I stopped to look around. There was a spirit somewhere and from the amount of nausea I felt, I knew it was going to be bad. Looking past all of the cars and trucks in the lot, I finally spotted it and wasn't prepared for what I saw. This spirit had gone too far and what used to be a woman now looked like a demon. That wasn't even the worst part, that was the fact that she was attached to a guy. Her arms and legs hooked to his back with what looked like tree roots.

His gait told me that this had been going on for a while because he limped and I could see from over here that he was pale and drawn. Before I could stop myself, I ran over causing nausea to double, but I couldn't stop. I was probably the only person in this whole town that could help him. There was no way I could do anything but that.

He fell as I neared and my steps got quicker. The need to help him riding me because he looked close to death. His pale skin shined in the sun and his blue eyes were tired. As soon as I was to him, I gritted my teeth as I put out a hand to help him up.

"Sorry about that sometimes my legs don't want to

work." He said with a smile which caused me to frown. Dropping his hand, I stepped back and shot him a look.

"So what did you do to make her attach to you?" I asked, curious because, in all my seventeen years, I had never seen anything like this. His face looked confused by my question.

"What are you talking about?" His voice sounded sincere, but he had to know right? There was no way a spirit had gotten so attached to him without any one around here noticing.

"The spirit that is attached to you. She is right on your back. By the look of you, she has been there a while. Haven't you felt her literally sucking the life out of you?" I said as I turned my head and looked at her. This close I could see that she was very aware and her red eyes flashed.

He's mine! You can never have him! I will get my revenge by helping rid the world of his bloodline. The ghost's voice yelled and I was brought to my knees by the sheer malevolence in it. Evil soaked into my pores and it felt hard to breathe.

"That's what is wrong with me? Do you really see a ghost? Is that why I'm so sick? Can you help me?" The hopefulness in his eyes almost broke me. Who knew how long this had been going on?

Before I could pull myself up, my eyes locked with the ghosts. They were as deep as endless pits and it felt as though she was trying to pull me in. My Uncle's voice shattered the trance I had been in.

"Kat!!!! Damn it will you answer me. I am trying to help you." Remembering my Uncle was behind me I shrugged looking over indicating he could continue.

"Thank you. Now repeat after me and the ghost will become visible. He will see what has been killing him and it may help the town form a different opinion on people like you. Go stand as close to him as you can. Try to grab his hand and say these words. 'Spiritus aperio tuus se.'" My uncle said the fear in his voice was evident and I wasted no time to do exactly what he said. If he was worried about this ghost she had to be evil.

Grabbing the guy's hands, I quickly shout "Spiritus aperio tuus se." The words barely left my mouth when a rock hard body collided with mine. Knocking me off my feet, I slammed into the ground. My eyes popped open just as giant hands.

"You leave him alone! Fucking Necro's always up to no good! I don't care if you are my mate, you will never take him! I will kill you first." The hands around my throat stopped the world around me. Everything blurred but I couldn't let him die. The sound of voices filled me with hope someone would help.

"Cass, what the fuck is that on Luke? What do we do?" With those words, the pressure on my throat was gone. Opening my eyes, I saw that my Uncle had knocked the man off me.

Not paying attention to any of the yelling or fighting, I slinked over to Luke while they were distracted and took his hand. His eyes were pleading and I had to save him.

"Relinquo nunc licet tu ambustum infernum!" I yelled and backed away as the ghost screamed. Everyone around us went still, including my Uncle, as the ghost looked like it was ripped from Luke's back. He fell to the ground, but my eyes were locked on hers as I watched the fire start at the bottom of her feet and work its way up.

You can't stop us. They will come for you! Were her last words as she exploded into nothingness. For a minute there was nothing but silence, but my uncle fixed that.

"Kitty kat, are you okay? I am going to kill him!" He asked as he came up beside me. I could hear the sound of guys talking and saw three guys and the dickhead move over to Luke, before turning my full attention to my Uncle.

"Yeah, I am, just tired. This is not how I expected my first day to go." I replied before turning around hoping that I could make a quick exit.

"Okay good, now I am going to go kill him!" He yelled, catching the attention of the guys. His anger slammed into me and I knew I wouldn't be getting away anytime soon.

"Just leave it! I want to go home." I said giving it one last shot for us to get the hell out of here. However, one of the guys left the pack and came over to me.

"What the hell just happened? Sorry to bother you, but I need to know what that was?" He said, his violet eyes piercing me. I had never had to explain this to another person before.

"Jake! Get the fuck away from her. She's a filthy necro and you have no idea what she can do. Just because she got rid of one ghost doesn't mean we can trust her. It was probably her that sent that thing to attack Luke in the first place. She even comes with her own personal asshole ghost protector. You fucking saw what he did to me." The Jake guy just shook his head before turning to look at the remaining two guys sitting with Luke.

"Take him back to the house. I will call Dr. Edwards and have him come check Luke over." Turning back to me as the two other guys lifted Luke into the waiting car, he smiled before continuing.

"Ignore my friend there, pretty lady, he was raised with wolves and doesn't know better. Thank you for helping Luke. He has been sick for a long time and I am hopeful whatever you did helped him as he smells a little different now. However, as you can understand me, his family, and his friends...well we have some questions so if it's okay with your very angry looking friend would you accompany us back to the house so we can talk."

"Fuck no, she's leaving! She's had enough for one day. Abused, shouted at, rejected by her mate, faced a demonic ghost, attacked by a neanderthal, who I will be dealing with by the way. No, she won't be going anywhere with you." My Uncle yelled and while I understand they have questions. I just want to go home. It's been a long day, but I have a feeling they won't take no for an answer.

"Rejected by her mate? Rejected by her fucking mate! What the fuck Cass? You rejected our mate without talking to us about it? How could you do that?" Oh hell no Jake was crazy and this was my cue to get the fuck out of here.

"Thanks but no thanks. I had one mate reject me, I don't want another. If Luke doesn't get better then you can contact my Grandfather. He's a vampire too so you shouldn't have too much trouble tracking him down." With that, I turned on my heel leaving the school, the guys, and the day behind me. I knew my Uncle wanted to say something but thankfully, he stayed quiet before finally disappearing. We would talk about that later too but for now, I needed my Nona, she would know how to fix this mess.

Chapter Seven

ASH

"Anybody know exactly what just happened?" I asked. We were all in the living room and had just listened to the doctor give Luke a full clean bill of health. While that was something we had all wished for I was waiting for the other shoe to drop.

"That fucking Necro.." Cass started but was cut off when Jake sped over and got in his face.

"That fucking Necro just saved our best friend's ass. He is going to live now because of her. You selfish bastard! Not only did you ruin your chance at happiness. You ruined mine!" Jake screamed before stepping back.

It was strange seeing him so worked up because he was usually the voice of reason. Ironic that the Vampire was the calm one out of us all. Cass was the typical Alpha male wolf, he was always right even when he wasn't. Klaus was a special breed half mage, half shifter, his mood swings were erratic, to say the least. Luke as the only human had been sick for so long I couldn't remember what he was like before. Then there was me quiet, stubborn but lethal when pushed. Typical Gargoyle.

"What happened when we left? And keep it the fuck down Luke is trying to sleep. He may be ok now, but he's been through hell. Let him fucking rest." Klaus glared at the others. I hated the tension. We were brothers. No matter what our fucked up families did, we always had each other but this girl came along and everything was messed up. Pushing his hands through his hair, Jake sighed before sitting on his favorite chair.

"You know how that psychic told us we would all have the same mate? Well, Mr. Genius over here went and rejected her and now she hates us. For a few seconds, I thought we had it all. Luke was going to be okay and we had met our mate, but now that's all gone. And he doesn't care." As Jake leaped up going towards Cass again, I stepped between them.

"Who is this girl? She may be our mate but so far, all she has done is cause us to fight each other. Something, I might add, that has never happened before. Is some slut really worth that?" A look of pure rage flashed across Jake's face and I knew I fucked up, but before anything happened the man that had been there with the Necro girl was standing before us. A dark sinister smile spread across his face as he spoke.

"Now boys I think it's time for us to have a little chat don't you?"

And He Killed Them All!!!!
Or Did He?
FIND OUT SOON :)

Alexis Taylor

Alexis is a mother of three demons, from a small town where nothing ever really happens outside of a writer's mind. A huge lover of books, she started to follow her favorite indie authors on social media two years later she alongside her best friend decided it was time to share the crazy dark stories from their minds with the world. Publishing Terror in a friend's anthology their love for writing was born.

A huge lover of the Supernatural, and all things dark and twisted, she has big plans for future stories and will never stick to just one genre or trope. Now signed to BBB Publishings and a featured Romance Lovers Author the next few years will be filled with exciting new worlds, stories, and definitely some more Twisted Rejections.

A self-proclaimed snobby reader she vows to give her readers different, engaging stories that push the boundaries of the normal author. Never one to back down from a challenge Alexis is one of her and her co-authors biggest critics, always determined to be better and do more her fans are definitely in for a treat.

When she isn't busy with her children, working, or writing she will usually be stalking cover groups for pretties or trolling Instagram for inspiration. If you want to keep up with Alexis, come stalk her by clicking on the link below. She loves nothing more than discussing books and ideas with like-minded readers. Plus she has a serious addiction to giving swag, and other goodies away.

https://linktr.ee/AlexisTaylorAuthor

Other Books by Alexis Taylor

HELL'S WRATH SERIES

Waking the Demon Within

Heart Of Stone

Twisted A Rejected Mates Series

Goddess Of Trickery: Blood Moon Series

Shorts and anthology stories

Terror
Unleashed
Rites Of Passion
Christmas Miracle
BBB Academy (Found in Relentless A bully Romance Collections)
Infernum Academy (Found in Relentless A bully Romance Collection)
Twisted Secret Part One (Found In Twisted Rejection Anthology)
Twisted Secret Part Two (Found In Twisted Rejection Part Two Anthology)
Fractured Minds (Found In The Anthology Tales Of All Hallows Eve)
Silversen Sisters: Minnies's Return (Found In The My Villainous Ways Anthology)
Anonymous Part 2 (Can you guess which story is by Alexis?)

Haunted Kind Of Love

BY: EVELYN BELLE

Ghost Level

For my Nana.
Who I know would be a nature witch
and guides me to this day.

Chapter One

It was exactly the same. The cottage on the outskirts of the small town. Grandma's escape. She came here when grandpa went hunting with the boys. Or fishing. Really, whenever grandpa left the house, so did she. And sometimes when he was still in the house, just to have some time away from his sports. Grandma loved nature in the purest form. The forest. The sounds of the stream that babbled over the rocks behind the cottage. The smell of the trees when the breeze blew gently through them. She adored it all.

The wide porch of the cottage still had the seashell wind chimes she had made, hanging from the beams. The walkway that grandpa had insisted be laid with paving stones in their golden years, so grandma didn't fall and hurt herself, lined with all the rocks she collected over the years. Large, small, glimmering white, dark colors. No two the same. She liked things different. Everything has its own personality, she would say.

Moss, that grandpa complained about, growing across the roof still clung to it. Grandma won that battle. We knew she would. The ivy we planted on both sides of the porch when I was five, had grown and taken on a life of its own. Spreading across the porch railing and clinging to the sides of the house. The white and pink flowers that bloomed in spring on it starting to appear in the green foliage.

Her cottage was mine now.

When she died last year, my grandparents left my dad the house in the will. Even though he grew up in the house, he couldn't bring himself to move into it. It's a rental now. A home to a very lovely family with small children that will create chaos and memories. My grandma would approve of it. My dad's siblings weren't surprised the house was left to him. He gave them the opportunity to move into it if any of them wanted to. No one did.

There are five children from my grandparents, eighteen grandchildren. There was a bit of commotion when some of the others found out I was getting grandma's cottage, but it was quickly quieted by their parents. I was the oldest of them all. I spent the most time with my grandparents, even towards the end of their lives. I spent the most time with grandma at the cottage. The other grandchildren saw it as an investment, something to be turned into a rental, but not me.

It was now my escape. The break up wasn't bad, but the stalking afterwards, that was a bit much. He would show up at my job, at my gym, at the grocery store when I was shopping. It wasn't random. It was definitely stalking. Even the police agreed when I called them after catching him sitting outside my townhouse, for the fourth night in a row. I was granted a restraining order, but the police suggested that maybe getting out of town for a bit would be a good idea. I wasn't going to argue.

So that's why, I'm sitting in front of my newly inherited

cottage, with one of my grandma's favorite tea cups filled with lavender tea, watching the movers I hired bring furniture from my grandparents house into the cottage. A plumber was checking all the pipes in and under the house. No plumbing issues, please. I smiled, watching the painter fight a particularly stubborn vine of ivy, that doesn't seem to want him to touch up the white railing of the porch. Grandma kept the cottage in perfect shape, but if I was going to be staying here through spring and summer, possibly into the beginning of fall, I was going to be sure I didn't need to call anyone out.

The sun was shining through the trees around the cottage and soon it would be warming the front yard, giving the ground the energy it needed to make all grandma's bulbs come up. I pushed back on my toes in the swing that hung from the oak tree. My flats digging into the grass beneath them. Yesterday, the gardener I found in town came by and planted my new addition to the cottage. Roses. I had an arbor added to the start of the walkway to the house, the roses planted beside it. Climbing roses were added today by the gardener's son, who would be here twice a month to check on the garden and tend to the lawn, if needed. While grandma had a green thumb, mine was black. Nothing survived.

Tea cup empty, I stood to head into the cottage to see if I was needed for arranging things. I told them where I wanted things, but that was a while ago and I probably spoke far too quickly in my excitement. Walking across the lawn I paused to look beyond the back of the cottage. There was a path, faint and overgrown, almost forgotten but not quite, that ran into the forest. There was a pull there, something wanted me to come explore.

"Ms. Baker." My name pulled me from the forests captivating grasp and back to reality.

I turned my eyes to the porch where one of the movers stood smiling. "Yes, I'm coming."

"Sorry to bother you, Ms. Baker," He began as I approached the steps.

"Victoria." I reminded him as I climbed the three steps to the porch.

"Yes, right, Victoria. Well, you see, we have a problem." He gave me a smile that said it wasn't really a problem.

"Which piece doesn't fit in which doorway?" I asked turning towards the kitchen wanting to put my cup down.

"The large dresser. The dark brown one. You wanted it in the back bedroom but it won't make the turn in the hallway." He waited in the doorway of the kitchen as I set the cup in the sink.

"You mean to tell me, you got that dresser all the way up the stairs, and it won't turn?" I felt the frown pinch my brow.

"Yes ma'am." He wiped the back of his hand across his forehead, clearly I was an intimidating woman from the city.

"It will fit. Come on. Let's go have a look." I replied walking towards the stairs, shedding the sweater I was wearing to fight off the morning chill.

I moved up the stairs to find the other two movers staring at the dresser as if it was a mortal enemy. I suppose it was. It was holding up their job. The large dresser was my grandmothers, it was passed down from her mother to her, and her grandmother to her mother, and so on. It was brought over from somewhere overseas and it was now a family heirloom. An heirloom that seemed to be making these guys a bit perturbed.

"Could I have one of the moving blankets please?" I held my hand out and one of them passed me a thick cloth blanket. I laid it on the floor before asking, "Tip it on its side now if you would."

With a shrug the three movers began to guide the dresser onto its side on top of the blanket. I waited till they stepped back before moving around and unscrewing the thick feet of the dresser. Each one was intricately designed and none of them the same. With all four feet in hand I slipped past them and set them on the foot of the bed.

"Alright, let's give it a try now." I moved to the corner of the room to be out of the way and watched as the dresser turned the corner slipping effortlessly into the room. I smiled at the mover who shook his head. "See. It fit."

"You could have just told us the feet came off." He smiled at me as I walked past the pair reattaching the feet.

"Now where would the fun have been in that?" I asked with a smile before turning to head back down the stairs.

The living room was piled high with boxes. I had emptied my townhouse of most of my belongings. Furniture stayed behind and the decor. My dad was going to have it cleaned before putting it up on a travel site for people to rent. It was in a good area of the city, close to a lot of the things tourists like to see. I just hoped my ex didn't bother the renters. That would be an awkward conversation to have.

I had inheritance money from my grandparents tucked away in a separate account from the money I brought in for work. One of the nice things about doing what I do, my work travels with me. The town is small, but not too small for Wi-Fi. The signal isn't too great at the cottage and I'm sure my grandma would just be terribly upset if she knew I had it put in, but I have to work and I need the Wi-Fi. I had already decided that once a week I would make a trip to one of the coffee shops in town to use their stronger Wi-Fi for anything I needed to upload.

I opened one of the boxes thinking I would start putting things away but a commotion out front followed by a slight scream of terror, drew me from that task. I smiled to myself as I closed the box and stepped onto the porch. I was greeted by the painter flat on his back staring daggers at my ivy. Today was going to be eventful.

By evening everything was moved into the house. The plumber said all the pipes looked good but if I decided to renovate, it wouldn't hurt to replace the pipes. Noted sir. The painter won his battle with the ivy and only left with a few extra swipes of white paint across his face. The ivy had something against him. While making dinner I decided to check my emails. Nothing too interesting, my boss telling me I need to think about taking some of the vacation time I've racked up. Nothing pressing.

That meant my weekend was free and that box I opened earlier had something in it I was itching to get my hands on. My camera. That trail that led into the woods was going to get explored tomorrow and the camera was coming along for the adventure. I decided I would go through two boxes tonight, one being the box my camera was in. A plan in motion, I turned back to my dinner and sat down at the table like my grandma would have liked.

The next morning I got dressed, slipped on my hiking boots, tossed some water and snacks in a backpack before checking to be sure the batteries for the camera charged overnight. Green light means go. I returned the batteries to the camera and clicked the power button, smiling at the sound it made when turning on. I had checked the camera card the night before and cleared off some horrid pictures before replacing it. I was ready for this adventure, whatever it might be.

I stepped out the front door, locking it behind me, before taking off down the trail that had taunted me the day before. It was more overgrown than it looked from the front yard. I picked my way across the trail, smashing down broken twigs with my boots and stepping over falling branches. Even as overgrown as the trail was it had a clear direction. I headed deeper into the forest, soon I couldn't even hear the sound of the little stream, just the sound of my feet crunching leaves.

I stopped a few times to take some pictures when something caught my eye, but I didn't wander off the trail. Something didn't feel right about it. A couple times I stopped to look behind me, it felt like someone else was walking the same path I was, no one was there but I could have sworn someone was. I pushed on, that pull dragging me deeper into the forest. Something was calling to me.

About half an hour into the walk a clearing opened up and I stopped in my tracks. It was a beautiful house, run down and overgrown, as if the forest was reclaiming its land. But that didn't cover the beauty the house was. I took several photos almost before realizing I was doing it. I wandered close to the front of the house, continuing to take the photos, but that feeling was there again. Something wasn't right.

"I hope it's alright that I'm taking photos." I said the words aloud, as if someone would give me permission, and as soon as I did the feeling seeped away.

I stepped onto the property and noticed immediately that even though the house was run down, the garden and landscape didn't seem to change. Roses lined the wall, not in bloom yet, but they would be. I was sure bulbs were in the ground and working their way up for their spring reveal. I walked through the grounds with caution and care. Rounding a corner I saw a gazebo in one corner of the yard. I could imagine a young couple sitting there, years ago, chatting about the future and what it meant for them.

I stepped further around the corner and stopped. Statues were everywhere on this side of the house. Beautiful statues of angels and other things. Call me weird but statues have always given me a sense of foreboding. I didn't like them. I raised my camera to take a picture of the gazebo but didn't move further into that part of the house. No thank you, I'll pass on coming into your lair, creepy things. I took several pictures before backing out of the area with precise steps.

Once clear of the garden of horrors, I moved back to the front of the house. I wanted a picture of the entire front of the house, but I would have to move really far back. I positioned myself back, as far away from the house as the trail would let me, and I could swear the house seemed brighter as I snapped the picture. As if the sun had moved just right, to bring a new glow about it. I settled on a rock at the edge of the path before digging a water bottle from my backpack, and just admired the beauty of the house.

I had spent hours out there. Staring at the house, wondering who had lived there, what had happened to them. Taking more and more pictures, before I forced myself to take the trail back home. I showered when I got home and was currently sitting in the living room, with a cup of tea waiting for my camera to load the photos onto my laptop. I wanted to see how everything came out. The pictures started popping up and I eagerly opened them to slide through them. I was happily admiring them, sipping my tea, until I got to one of the pictures I took when I first saw the house, and I almost dropped my cup.

In the corner of the photo, there was a figure. A figure in all white that seemed to be walking toward the house. The house that I knew was empty. The house that I knew was being reclaimed by the forest. I set the cup down on the table before continuing through the photos. All of them were beautiful, until the chill ran over my skin again as I noticed the same white figure, walking away from the house this time.

"What in the everloving hell is that?" I mumbled to myself before I thought better. "You know what, I don't want to know."

But part of me did, because as I closed my laptop, I tucked the camera back into my backpack and put my hiking boots by the side of the couch. I was going back tomorrow, I just didn't realize it yet.

It wasn't just the next day that I went back to the house. I started itching to go back to the house every day. After I finished my work, I would tug on my boots and walk through the woods to the house. Some days I sat on the rocks away from the house and admired it for a short time, other days I took my camera and took more pictures of the house. I wasn't brave enough to go inside the house, it didn't feel right. Most of the days I took a notebook and kept track of how things made me feel. If looking at a particular part of the house made me feel uneasy, or if a part made me feel peaceful.

Some days I created a life for the house. I gave it a family. I gave it a past and a heritage. If you asked me why, I couldn't even begin to tell you, but the house called to me. A call so strong I could only imagine this was how a Siren's call would feel to a sailor. And as crazy as it sounded, I sometimes caught myself talking to the house, as if it would give me insight into what happened to it before I found it.

One day, a month or so later, it rained. It rained hard and I knew there would be no adventure to the house in the forest. Instead of venturing out, I decided to go through all the photos I had taken over that time. I sorted the photos by date and just started clicking through them. Soon, I noticed that white figure appeared in almost all the sets of pictures. One going towards the house and one leaving the house. I frowned looking at the pictures. I moved them, each one with the figure in it, into a separate folder.

I enhanced them, zoomed in on them, but nothing I did seemed to bring the figure into focus. I sat back on the couch and folded my arms over my chest, biting my thumb nail in thought. I shouldn't want to go back, but I was going too. I needed to know who this person was coming to the same house I did, without me seeing them.

The next day was clear, the blue sky above promised a warmer day than the day before. The path to the house was becoming more clear, with my constant trips to it. There were no longer branches or leaves. Everything was crunched down by my passes. As the house came into view I could feel the smile turning the corners of my mouth. Part of me realized that I was bordering on obsessed, the other part wasn't sure we cared. Today, I brought snacks, plenty of water and lunch. I wasn't planning to return home till I spotted this person coming or going from the house.

Hours passed, I snacked on some cashews and drank a bottle of water, without seeing another person. I had started to unpack my lunch when out of the corner of my eye I spotted the figure moving across the lawn of the house. I set my food down before sprinting across the dirt path that separated me from the house.

"Hey!" I called as I rounded the corner of the brick wall that surrounded the house.

But there was no one in sight. I felt the frown appear as the irritated feeling settled into my nerves. How can someone move that fast? I started to step onto the property but something felt wrong. I took several steps back feeling confused as the feeling disappeared the further I moved away. I gave the house a long look before turning back to my lunch. Dropping down onto the rock and pulling my sandwich from my bag, I didn't take my eyes off the house.

I had finished almost all my lunch and was about to give up on seeing the person again when I caught sight of the figure coming out the front door. I dropped my trash into my bag before standing up. I watched the person move towards the side of the house before I cupped my hands around my mouth to yell.

"Hey!" The figure slowed but didn't look at me, I raised my hands again. "Hey! Who are you?"

This time, the figure did stop and I couldn't help the chill that ran across my skin. I watched as they turned towards me and their features seemed to become clearer. I raised my hand in greeting, watching as the person returned the gesture. And at that moment, I realized I had no idea what to do next. What if this person was a murderer? What if the house was where they kept their victims? And my dumbass just made myself a perfect target. But what if they weren't. What if they were just members of the family that used to own the house, and they were coming here to see what the house was all about.

As the person started walking towards me, I was

hoping it was the second version rather than the first. I wasn't looking to be murdered in the middle of the forest. I hooked my thumbs in the pockets of my jeans, close to the small knife I kept there. I started carrying it when a friend of mine in the city was mugged, six times, in broad daylight. They could try for my bag, but I was taking some flesh for their troubles.

The closer the person came, the more it seemed like the fuzzy haze faded away, like they were walking out of a fog. I also started to notice that the person was a male and not dressed like any male I had seen in some time. He wore a suit, a well tailored suit. Dark color with a bright blue tie and a crisp white shirt beneath it. His shoes were shiny and he wore a hat as well. Definitely not dressed like the guys I was used to seeing.

"Hello." I said as he stopped a good distance from me.

"Hello as well. Are you visiting the McGillan's?" He asked, tucking his hands into his pockets.

"No, I just moved to town." I replied watching him glance around.

"Where is your escort?" He inquired.

"My what?" I raised a brow at the question.

"Your escort, where is he? Or are you out alone?" He seemed perplexed by my confusion.

"I don't have an escort. I am perfectly capable of walking the woods alone and handling myself." I felt my confusion double.

"Very modern, I must say. Your husband must feel comfortable with you out alone." He seemed to relax a little.

"Um, I don't have a husband. I'm not married." I replied, watching the confusion cross his face.

"Widowed?" He questioned.

"Such personal questions for a first meeting." I stated simply, watching his brows raise slowly.

"You are right. I apologize. It's just…" He paused looking back at the house. "I have seen you out here before, but wasn't sure I was actually seeing someone else." He turned back to look at me with a frown. "But you are definitely here and a person."

"Last time I checked I was." I rocked back on my heels for a second. "So, what are you doing way out here all by yourself?"

"I am visiting the McGillan's of course." He stated as if it made perfect sense.

"Of course you are. How silly of me." I replied.

"Well, I will leave you to, whatever you were doing. I must be off." He tipped his hat to me before turning and walking away from the direction I came from.

"Wait," I called turning to look at him as he glanced back. "What's your name?"

He glanced at the house for a split second before answering, "Leonard. Leonard Mills."

I made my way home that afternoon feeling less than accomplished. If anything, I had more questions about what happened that day. I had been in town a few times since moving in, mostly for groceries and had been to the bigger town not far away, and I hadn't seen Leonard in either of them. He could be from the bigger town and I hadn't seen him, but I doubted it. As I made my dinner that night, I couldn't help but think about how he was dressed and the way he talked.

I decided, halfway through eating, that I would go into town in the morning. I had some files that needed to be sent, so a trip to my favorite coffee shop was necessary anyway. While I was there, I would see if I could catch a glimpse of the stranger or see if anyone knew who he was.

Feeling better about having a plan of action, I headed to bed.

Laptop bag slung over my shoulder, I wandered into town. I was starting to learn people by name and greeted a few as I passed. Everyone was friendly in town, except the old lady that lived not far from my cottage. She always gave me such a nasty look and I had no idea why. I had decided not to engage with her again, after she had slammed her door as I said 'good morning' passing by. Clearly, I was not welcome.

Arriving at the coffee shop I could tell the normal morning rush was over. Only a few customers dotted the small interior. Most people in town grabbed a coffee before starting their commute to the larger surrounding towns or even further into the city. I walked up to the counter and was greeted by the usual barista behind the counter. Dean was a handsome guy. Dark hair with some of the brightest blue eyes I had ever seen. His smile was a million watt and could melt the polar caps. I had been in the shop to see him fend off the flocks of both younger and older women. Clearly he was spoken for.

"Hey Victoria!" That voice was like chocolate, sinful and delicious. "Your usual?"

"Hi Dean. How could you possibly know 'my usual' by now?" I used my fingers as air quotes before adjusting my bag.

"I have lived here for a while now, I know everyone in town. I know all their usuals and when they change for seasonal items. You are new. It's easy to memorize a new order." He smiled at me grabbing a cup from behind him.

"What if I changed my mind?" I asked, folding my arms over my chest.

"That's why I asked if you would have your usual." I knew it wasn't possible but it seemed like his smile got brighter.

"Smart guy. Yes, my usual." I pulled my card from my pocket as he tapped the screen before him.

My coffee and pastry paid for, I walked out onto the patio to sit in the sun. Settling into the chair facing towards where my cottage would be, I set up my laptop and connected to the Wi-Fi. My boss was expecting two of these files, so the other three would be a surprise and earn me some quiet time over the next week. Which I planned to use to stalk the house, or rather the stranger who visited the house.

Dean brought my coffee and pastry out as I was uploading the first file. I thanked him and without a single ounce of remorse, watched him walk back into the coffee shop as I sipped my coffee. I wasn't interested in a relationship at the moment, but that didn't mean I couldn't appreciate good looking people. Dean definitely fell in that category.

An hour later the few customers that had been in the shop went on their way and I was the only person left hanging around. I was uploading the fourth file when my coffee cup was replaced with a new one. I looked up to see Dean standing beside me holding the empty cup.

"You're here longer than normal." He stated.

"I had extra files to send to the boss. Am I bothering you?" I asked.

"Nope." He turned and tossed the empty cup in the trash before flopping himself into the chair next to mine. "You're usually pretty quick. I don't think I've ever seen you finish a coffee here."

"I finish them walking home." I responded, glancing at the bar on the screen.

"I kinda figured that." His grin made my heart do a little skip. "Don't you have the internet at your place?"

"I do, but it isn't strong enough to upload these files. Don't ask me why, it just doesn't like working that much." I smiled, raising the cup to my lips.

"I should thank it. I like seeing you in here." I could have sworn I saw color flush his cheeks. "I mean, I like seeing all my customers."

"I bet you say that to all the city girls." I raised my brows at him before setting the cup down.

He laughed before shaking his head. "There was a time when I did, but that is a story for another day."

"Like a day when you aren't supposed to be working." I glanced at the coffee shop door as a pair of women pulled the door open walking inside.

"Yeah, I guess so." He stood from the chair with a huff. "Maybe we can have lunch some day and I'll tell you my tale of woe."

"That doesn't sound like a terrible idea." I said, watching him nod and head towards the door.

"I'm going to hold you to that." He pointed a finger at me before slipping back into the coffee shop.

I looked back at the laptop before moving the last file to be uploaded. I knew Dean wouldn't be back out before this one was done. Those two women were going to talk his ear off while he smiled and nodded. Dean was a flirt, but a harmless flirt. I sipped the coffee waiting for the last file to finish. When it did, I closed everything up and packed it away. When I waved to Dean as I walked down the street, he was still standing at the counter talking to the two women who had not moved to a seat. Poor guy. It wasn't till I got home that I realized I had forgotten to ask about

Leonard. I stopped at the fence to my cottage and allowed myself the face palm I deserved. I guess I was going to have to take up Dean on his lunch offer after all.

I wasn't able to get out to the house for a few days after that, but when I did Leonard was there again. I waved to him but didn't stop him like I did before. He waved tentatively and glanced back at the house again, before disappearing down the lane away from town. This continued for a few weeks. I would wave and he would sort of wave back. By the end of a month, he started waving to me first and even smiled a time or two.

Spring was moving quickly into summer and the days were becoming beautifully warm. I had seen Leonard at the house every other day. He had even come over and had a normal conversation, meaning one that didn't involve him asking why I was alone. I had offered him some of my snacks but he assured me that he would be fine till he arrived home. When I asked him where home was, he had pointed down the lane that was overgrown and going away from town. It seemed odd to me, but he seemed sure of the direction and his confident smile made me feel silly to think about questioning him.

I was standing in my room staring at the three different outfits I had picked out for my lunch with Dean, yes it took us that long to find a date where he wasn't working and I wasn't swamped, when a dress in the corner of the closet caught my eye. It wasn't one of mine and I couldn't be completely sure it wasn't there when I unpacked my things. I pulled the dress out and admired it. It had to be one of grandma's from when she was younger. A thought crossed my mind and brought a smile to my lips. I decided to wear it next time I went to the house. I bet Leonard would chuckle.

Blinking, I hung the dress back up. Why would I care what he thought of how I dressed? I gave myself a little shake and went back to picking out what I would wear to lunch. I grabbed the skirt and top I had picked first, dressed quickly and hurried out the front door. Walking past the house next to mine, I caught sight of the old lady as she peeked out of her window.

Dean was standing in front of the diner he had picked out. When I told him I hadn't tried any of the food places in town, I could have sworn his eyes were going to bug out of his head. He said this was where we would go. I couldn't argue with him since I didn't have a better suggestion.

"Damn, you look amazing." He said as I walked up to him.

"Um, thank you. Is it because I put on makeup?" I asked, raising my brow at him.

"You put on makeup?" He bent closer and squinted at me. "Oh yeah, I guess you did."

I pushed him away stifling the giggle that threatened. "Don't be weird."

"Sweetie, weird is my middle name. So is coffee and cake and donut. Mmmm, I love donuts." He patted his midsection where there was clearly no indication of such a love.

"Sure you do. So, are we going in to eat or what? I'm starving out here." I motioned to the door.

"Oh yes, this place has the best burgers in town." He replied holding the door open.

"Burgers? Really?" I asked as I passed under his arm.

"Trust me, you'll thank me later." He said with his signature grin.

He wasn't lying. The burgers were pretty dang good.

Cooked perfectly and piled high with all the goodies. What he didn't tell me was that his mother owned the place and had been cooking there since she opened it when he was five. She was a funny lady, who had zero reservations about teasing her son. It was clear where Dean got his personality from. When she slid two plates onto the table with cake on them, I was pretty sure I loved her.

"You didn't tell me you grew up here." I pointed a cake coated fork at Dean as he shoved a bite in his mouth.

I watched him smile as he chewed and swallowed the bite. "You never asked."

"Good point." I nodded poking at the cake again. "But you said before that there was a time you said something to all the girls. Did you leave town for a while? You said that was a story for another time."

"You have a good memory. I'm not sure I like that." He pointed his own fork at me in accusation before taking another bite. "I left town after high school. I moved to the city and tried to make my way there. I did odd jobs while I went to college. One of those jobs was a barista at a coffee shop inside a high end hotel. I made good tips if I paid good compliments. I learned soon who the regulars were, even in the city at a hotel they have them." His smile faltered a little as he pushed the frosting from the cake around the plate for a second. "I had one customer, beautiful lady, she would come in weekly. Then it became every other day. Then daily. Finally she asked me out for drinks." He set the fork down but kept staring at the plate. "She was married. She was using me to make her husband, who was having an affair, jealous. And it worked." He sighed heavily before looking up at me. "We were having drinks and she leaned in kissing me. I definitely didn't fight it but the right hook that caught me a second later did make me think I should have. Her husband had followed her and clocked me good. They started fighting, causing a scene and I took the opportunity to split." He touched his jaw almost subconsciously. "After that I decided the city wasn't for me. I finished school and came back home. I rent the little apartment above the coffee shop and keep a low profile."

"Sounds like you got used. I'm so sorry." I reached across the table and covered his hand with mine. "Not all city girls are like that."

He rolled his hand beneath mind before brushing his thumb across my knuckles. "You kinda showed me that."

I felt the blush rise and pulled my hand back, picking up my fork again. "Well, I'm glad to have helped."

"What about you? What made you leave the city? If you don't mind me asking." He pushed his plate away from him before crossing his arms on the table top.

"An ex-boyfriend. He didn't know what 'no' meant and it was time for me to remove myself from the situation for a bit. My grandma died and left the cottage to me. Seemed like the perfect time to do a little soul searching and get away at the same time." I smiled at him as I polished off the cake.

"I like her." A voice from beside us announced, causing us both to look up. "She didn't bat an eye at finishing a burger, fries and cake. I'm keeping her if you don't."

Dean looked at his mom, mouth hanging open as she cleared the plates from in front of us. I leaned back in the seat, covering my smile with my hand. When the shock seemed to fade from his face, he looked at me again and I remembered to ask him about Leonard.

"So, I have a weird question." I leaned on the table.

"I don't watch chick flicks." He shook his head.

"Neither do I, but that's not the question." I blinked once before tilting my head. "Wait, what?"

"I thought you were going to ask if I wanted to watch some chick flick with you." He responded with a smile.

"No chick flicks." I shook my head. "Anyway, do you know anyone by the name of Leonard Mills?"

Dean's brows pressed together in a frown. "The name doesn't sound familiar. Why?"

I told him about the path behind my cottage. The house tucked in the woods. The creepy garden statues that I avoided. And finally about Leonard. When I was finished talking he leaned back in his seat and tapped a finger to his lips.

"I really can't think of anyone named Leonard. Even back in school, I don't think I knew of anyone named that, and our school is pretty small." He shook his head.

I felt my shoulders sag. "I was hoping you might know him."

"I could come with you one day. Maybe he is giving you a false name. If I saw what he looked like, maybe I could place him." Dean offered.

Something inside me bristled. "No, it's okay. I suppose it doesn't matter that much."

"I could ask my mom. Maybe she knows something or knows someone in town who might." Dean suggested.

"That might be something." I mumbled to myself.

Dean reached across the table and tipped my chin up. My eyes landed on those blue pools and he smiled. I smiled back, I just couldn't help it. Even after all the crap my ex had done, even after saying I was going to better myself, here I was getting butterflies with not one but two guys. And that thought carried me all the way back home after lunch. How could I have butterflies for someone I didn't even know?

I stared at myself in the mirror. I felt weird in the dress and to think, I was going to be walking through the forest in it. Since I had all but beaten back the dead branches and shrubs with my trips back and forth, it wouldn't be a problem to walk the short distance in a dress. I slipped the flats on before checking how I looked again. One time, I would give this one chance. If I fell, or tripped, or if a stump looked at me wrong, it was back to my boots.

I made my way through the forest, no incidents to report. I made it to the house and stopped to just stare at it. Did it seem a bit darker today? I glanced down the path towards my cottage before looking back again. It did seem darker. I frowned but still pulled the blanket from my bag. Spreading it on the ground I settled down with the lunch I had brought. Not long after, from the corner of my eye, I spotted Leonard walking towards the house.

He started to raise his hand in greeting but paused. He turned and started towards me. That was not his usual route. I set my sandwich down and stood up, brushing off my dress. He stopped at the edge of the blanket and looked at me for another second before speaking.

"You look nice. Very nice." His cheeks colored slightly before he cleared his throat.

"I found it in my closet. I," Catching myself before I said I thought he would like it. "I thought it would be a nice change."

"It is a change and not a bad one." He motioned for me to sit back down. "Please don't let me stop you from finishing your lunch."

I glanced back at the half eaten sandwich and fruit waiting for me. "Would you like to join me? I don't have another sandwich, but I wouldn't be opposed to sharing my fruit."

"I would like that." There was zero hesitation as Leonard sat down on the blanket.

I settled back onto the blanket, making sure to tuck the dress around my knees. I continued eating my sandwich, after offering Leonard some of the fruit. He took a grape and looked at it for a moment before popping it into his mouth. He leaned back on his palms staring at the house before us.

We made small talk. I asked about where he lived. He described a house I was sure I had seen before but brushed it off as his descriptive skills being that good. He asked about where I lived and I told him about the cottage. The frown tugged at his brows before disappearing again. I asked him why he came to the house everyday and he leaned forward sighing.

"To see my fiance." He replied looking towards the house.

"Your fiance is there?" I pointed at the house as he nodded.

"We are supposed to be married in the fall. I'm trying my hardest to get to know her." He sighed again.

I looked at the house again. The ivy was growing out of control and the forest seemed to be trying to take over one side of the house. While the grounds had seemed sort of tended to when I saw them the first time I walked there, the house seemed to be in disrepair. How could anyone be living there?

"Gwen McGillan. She is a bit older than me, but" He pursed his lips before looking at me. "Nevermind. It isn't proper for me to speak ill of anyone, let alone the person I'm supposed to be marrying."

"You don't seem so sure." I put the containers I had brought the food in back into my bag. "Do you not love her?"

He wrinkled his nose before schooling his features again and standing from the blanket. "I should be getting inside. She won't be happy that I'm late."

I stood from the blanket. "I should head home anyway. Thank you for sitting with me. It was nice talking to you."

"Thank you for allowing me. It's nice to talk to someone my age and not," He adjusted his tie and squared his shoulders. "I should go."

"Of course." I reached down for the blanket and started folding it. "Leonard?" He paused looking back at me. "Would you like to meet tomorrow again? I can bring more grapes since you seemed to like them so much."

The smile lifted the corner of his mouth. "I would really like that."

"Tomorrow then." I folded the blanket and tucked it into the bag, before turning down the path.

I wasn't going to give him an out. He said he would like it, I was going to hold him to it. I walked down the path but I could feel eyes on my back. Not just one pair, but a couple. I refused to glance back. I felt accomplished. I felt happy. I was going to relish in that feeling. I felt so good, I almost skipped. I stepped across the small stream behind the cottage and stopped quickly when I saw the old lady from next door standing at my gate. She didn't say anything, just stared at me before turning and shuffling back towards her house.

I panicked only a little when someone knocked at my door an hour later. I opened the door and smiled when I saw Dean standing there. I leaned against the door as his eyes took in the dress I was still wearing.

"You didn't have to get dressed up for me." He smiled at me, flicking his eyebrows up.

"I didn't know you were coming over, how would I have known to get dressed up?" I gave him a look.

"Point taken." He held out a potted plant. "This is for you. From my mom."

"From your mom?" I asked, taking the plant.

"Yeah, she likes what you are doing with the yard here. She said it needed a lily." He rocked back on his heels.

"Um, I don't really." I made a face looking at the plant. "I'm afraid if I kill it, which chances are very high that I will, your mom is going to be mad."

"Nah, she won't be mad." He stopped rocking for a second. "Wait, all your plants out front are flowering and blooming."

"Yeah, because the gardener takes care of them. I don't touch them." I looked at the lily again before an idea hit me. "Oh, I have an idea. Hold this."

I pushed the plant back into his hands, before slamming the door closed. I stopped halfway across the living room. Backtracking to the door, I yanked it open, reached out and dragged Dean inside by his shirt front.

"Wait here." I pointed to the living room before heading towards the stairs.

"Yes ma'am." Dean mumbled.

"I heard that." I called as I topped the stairs.

I changed into jeans, tossing the dress into the laundry before pulling a shirt from the closet and tugging it over my head. Pulling on my slip ons, I grabbed a rubber band from the dresser top as I left the room. Heading down the stairs I stopped at the bottom to see Dean right where I left him.

"You said wait here. I waited here." He pointed at the spot he was still standing in.

"Good to know you follow directions well. You are now on my apocalypse team." I pointed at him as I pulled my hair into a ponytail.

"Apocalypse team?" He looked down at the plant. "I just came to deliver a plant."

"Accept it. You look capable and you take what I say without lip. You're in now." I snatched the plant back from his hands as I started for the door. "Come on."

To his credit, Dean only looked slightly confused as he followed me across the porch and lawn. When I handed him the garden gloves I had snatched from the porch he raised a brow at me. I returned the look and he muttered under his breath before pulling them on. He planted the lily for me near where the other bulbs were already thriving. When he stood up and removed the gloves, he looked at me.

"Okay, I'll ask. Why did I have to plant the plant my mom sent for you?" He asked, folding his arms over his chest after gesturing to the new plant.

"Because if I had planted it, the thing would have died. Since you planted it, and the gardener tends to them, it has a much higher survival rate." I smiled tapping the dirty gloves against my palm.

He opened his mouth to say something before stopping to press a finger to his lips. "You know what, that makes sense. It's a bit weird and I'm starting to get the feel that you might be superstitious, but it makes sense."

"I am not superstitious. I am very open minded." I turned to head back to the house. "I come from a long line of supposed witches, don't you know?"

"Ah, that explains what mom was talking about." He replied when I was about halfway to the house.

"Excuse me?" I turned, putting my hands on my hips. "You want to explain that statement?"

He shrugged one shoulder like it wasn't really important, clearly trying to get a rise from me. "Just what old lady Johnson said last time mom delivered her food."

"Old lady Johnson?" I inquired with a raise of my brow.

He inclined his head towards the house next door, causally slipping his hands into the back pockets of his jeans. "Old lady Johnson."

"Oh, her." I shrugged my shoulders folding my arms over my chest. "She seems to have some sort of issue with me. I tried to be polite, but she doesn't seem to want any of that." I frowned. "In fact, she was standing at my gate this afternoon."

"Probably because she thinks you're a witch. She thought your grandmother was one as well. She has a pretty strong dislike for both of you, but more so for your grandma." Dean tilted his head watching me take in the information. "No comment?"

"I'm not a witch. If I was, I wouldn't have needed you to plant my lily." I tossed a smile at him before crossing the yard to the house and closing the door behind me. "A witch indeed. If I was a witch I wouldn't have so many questions."

I didn't see Dean again that day. The following day I pulled another dress from my closet and packed my lunch heading into the forest. I was starting to feel like Red Riding Hood, always wandering into the woods. When I stepped into the clearing where the house stood, Leonard was coming across from the other side. He smiled at me and my heart did a little extra thump in my chest.

He helped me unfold the blanket and sat down without

being asked this time. We chatted lightly about nothing in particular. Just enjoying the company. It was relaxed and peaceful. Even if it seemed like the house before us seemed even darker today. We parted ways an hour later and Leonard asked if he would see me the next day. Smiling, I agreed.

We continued like that for a week. Leonard was a friendly, wonderful companion. I found myself confessing things that I wouldn't tell anyone else. He listened and didn't try to fix my problem, sometimes he would offer advice that would make sense. Each day I would bring a little more food. Some more fruit, some cheese and crackers. When we packed everything up on that Friday, he leaned forward and pressed a kiss to my cheek. He looked as flushed as I felt when he stepped back.

As I walked back to my cottage I noticed two things. The house was definitely getting darker, looking more dangerous, and old lady Johnson was becoming a stalker. She shuffled away from my gate once more that day. As she had been every day for a week now. I climbed the steps to the cottage, stopping with my hand on the door. Something felt wrong.

Pushing open the door I felt the temperature shift. It seemed much cooler in my cottage than normal, especially since we were clearly in the middle of a very warm summer. I set my bag down by the door and crossed my doorway. The hair on my arm stood up suddenly. So suddenly I had to stop myself from turning away from my own house. Instead, I pushed my back against my door while I looked around the living room.

"I don't know who you are, but you were not invited in. Please leave or I will force you out." I spoke to an empty room.

Even as the words left my lips, I felt the air in the room

change. The pressing feeling that had been there was gone. The feeling of something being wrong left with whatever presence did. I closed my front door and leaned my head against it. I hadn't worried about someone breaking in, but whatever presence was here, was not welcome.

"What an awful time to not be a witch." I muttered.

I started to go change out of my dress before I decided it would be silly to change again to just go into town. I had a few things that I had been putting off doing, so now was a good time to do them. I grabbed my purse off the counter in the kitchen and locked the door behind me, before heading down the path to the gate.

I passed old lady Johnson's house and didn't even glance at her. Even though I could feel her staring at me. I stopped at the little post office we had in town, chatted with the very pregnant clerk at the counter before heading to the market in town. I stopped to get a coffee and was confused by my feelings when I didn't see Dean working. I was disappointed he wasn't there, even after he had tried to bait me. Calling me a witch, I should become one and turn him into a toad.

The thought made me smile as I pushed the door of the market open. Quietly browsing the shelves in the store, I was humming to myself when a whistle brought me from my thoughts. I glanced up and saw Dean in the next aisle. Part of me wanted to ignore him, but the other part of me reminded me that we were grown ass people. Damn.

"Hello." I said before continuing to browse.

"Wow." He blinked once with raised brows. "I must have really pissed you off."

"You did not piss me off." I responded quickly. "What would make you think you had?"

"Well," He skirted the end of the aisle and came to stop before me, one hand holding the carry basket from the market while the other got shoved in his pocket. "You haven't spoken to me in a week."

"I haven't seen you in a week." I reminded him, picking up a can from the shelf.

"And now you are having a hard time keeping eye contact with me, when at the diner you had no problem." He said plucking the can from my hand, before reading the label and making a face.

"Don't care for creamed corn?" I asked moving past him.

"Who creams corn?" He said, making a face. "But I was right, you are pissed at me."

I turned to face him and took a deep breath. "I am not pissed at you, but I am having a hard time with the idea that someone, especially an older person who knows nothing about me, thinks I am a witch."

"Ah, yeah, between you and me," He looked around like he was about to share a secret. "I thought it was kinda hot."

I would have liked to glare at him or make a snarky comeback, but instead those butterflies made themselves known and I smiled at him. "I really hate you."

"Oh yeah, I bet you say that to all the guys." He grinned at me.

"Actually, I do say that to a fair amount of them." I shrugged continuing down the aisle. "So, other than shopping, what are you doing here?"

"Shopping for essentials." He held up the basket allowing me to peek inside.

"Your mom owns a diner with amazing burgers and cake, and you're shopping for salad and pasta stuff?" I raised a brow at him.

"To be honest, I came in for beer." He shrugged. "But

then I saw you crossing the street and suddenly there are dinner makings in my basket. Weirdest thing."

"Strange shelves here at the market. People come in for beer and end up with dinner items. I'm shocked." I crossed an aisle and picked up a few apples before putting them in a bag.

"Maybe it was the universe giving me a hint," I met his blue eyes and felt that flutter again. "We could have dinner."

"You cook?" I questioned, picking out some strawberries.

"It's dry pasta, a jar of sauce and pre-packaged caesar salad, pretty sure even I could do this without messing it up." He looked slightly offended and I couldn't help the smile. "I could sweeten the offer and say we could watch a chick flick."

"Ew, no." I made a face before picking up some oranges and putting them in another bag. "What time, as long as there is no chick flick."

I noticed the way his shoulders relaxed. "Uh, how does six sound?"

"Six is good. Gives me time to get home and put stuff away." I picked up a bag of grapes checking them before they got added to the basket. "Can I bring anything?"

"Just your sexy ass." He smiled that million watt smile.

"Watch that mouth or I'll tell your mom." I replied pressing a finger into his chest, before heading to the front check out.

"You wouldn't tell her, would you?" The panic in his voice was definitely real.

Dinner ended up somehow being a disaster. When I arrived at six, Dean was fanning the smoke detector at the ceiling and giving me a death stare while I tried not to laugh. I helped open the windows around his living room that looked out over the main circle of town. Soon the smoke detector stopped it's horrible screeching and he attempted to look collected.

"What happened?" I asked, glancing at the kitchen that smelled like charred something.

"You know, let's just ignore that. I'm going to order takeout from the diner. My mom will be happy to feed you again." He pulled his phone from his pocket with a roll of his eyes.

I wandered the living room looking at the art that decorated his walls and smiled at the pictures of him and his mom. Behind me he was trying very hard to persuade his mom to not do something. His voice was becoming more irritated and more adorable, before I heard the groan of frustration and he cleared his throat. I stood from where I was admiring a picture that was very clearly of his high school prom. I held the picture up and he moved quickly across the room to take it from me.

"Let's not talk about that." He set it back where I picked it up from.

"I thought it was kinda adorable." I replied, turning to look at him.

"Uh huh." He turned back towards the kitchen. "Can I get you something to drink? Beer? Wine?"

"Just water please." I followed him towards the kitchen. "Can I help you clean up?"

He glanced at the stove before shaking his head. "Uh, no. I don't even know how to start cleaning that up."

"With soap and a trash can." I smiled as he handed me a bottle of water.

"Very funny. You are just full of helpful tips." He held a beer up before asking. "You don't mind, do you?"

"Not at all. Just because I'm not drinking, doesn't mean I don't." He nodded before twisting the top off the bottle and taking a sip. "Hey, did you happen to ask your mom about Leonard Mills?"

He made a motion as he finished the sip of his beer and set the bottle down. "Since you mentioned that, I did talk to her. She did know the name, but I don't know if you are going to like what I'm going to tell you."

I cracked the lid on the bottle of water before taking a sip. "I'm sure I'll survive."

"Mom said that someone did live in town by that name, almost 60 years ago. He died tragically when he was twenty." I frowned as he kept going. "So, I decided to ask around town for you. Since you don't know many people and I am the town heart throb." I rolled my eyes even as the smile appeared. "He is buried in the cemetery outside of town. Apparently, his family was wealthy at one time, but things took a turn and their finances weren't doing great. To help the family, Leonard proposed to a girl from a wealthy family, even though he was really in love with someone else."

I felt the smile slip from my lips as I set the water bottle on the counter. "He was going to marry someone he didn't love?"

"Tragic right? What dudes will do for their family." Dean shook his head before stopping himself. "Ya know, I would probably do it, if it kept my mom out of the poor house."

I licked my suddenly dry lips. "Did you find out what happened to him or the fiance?"

"Not much on the fiance, but Leonard was poisoned, at least his cause of death is poison. No one ever found out who did it." Dean leaned against the counter before looking at me. "Pretty crazy story, huh?"

"Yeah, pretty crazy." I repeated feeling my heart beat faster. "Did they say who the fiance was?"

"Oh, yeah, that was the part I found interesting. You know that house you said you have been going out to see, that was their place. The fiance lived there. What was the family name again?" He tapped a finger against his chin as he tipped his head back in thought.

"McGillan?" I almost whispered it.

"That's it!" He snapped his fingers before looking at me. "Wait, how did you know that?"

"Lucky guess?" I knew it didn't come across funny.

Dean set the bottle down. "Are you really seeing someone out there who thinks they are Leonard Mills?"

I nodded slowly, willing my heart rate to steady out. There was no way he was dead. We have lunch together. Ghosts can't eat, can they? I breathed in deeply through my nose and out slowly through my mouth, before picking up the bottle of water and taking a drink. Dean watched my face for a moment before stepping towards me.

"You okay?" He asked, putting his hands on my upper arms.

"Yeah, I'm okay. Someone is just playing a nasty joke on me is all." I shrugged, hoping Dean would take it as me accepting the joke.

"That is one terrible and well thought out joke." He frowned when there was a knock at the door. "Probably mom with the food. Are you still hungry?"

"Starving." I forced a smile and he dropped his hands to get the door.

His mom didn't wait for him to invite her in, she pushed past him holding two grocery bags. "I can't believe you tried to cook for her. Are you trying to kill her?"

"Mom, it was packaged pasta and bagged salad, it really should have been less cooking and more eating." Dean defended himself as his mom looked at the stovetop.

"I see how well that went over." She rolled her eyes, setting the bags on the counter before smiling at me. "Hungry Victoria, dear?"

"Starving actually. Did you see what he tried to feed me? I almost died." I put a hand to my chest in mock horror.

"Hey! I was destroying this before you arrived. I didn't even have time to try to kill you with it." Dean objected quickly.

"Well, don't worry. Mama bear will see you are fed now." She reached across the counter and patted my hand.

I couldn't hold the laugher anymore when Dean turned to his mom and called her a traitor. The only thing better was her comeback about me eating all the cake when he always left a bit of frosting. The argument that followed, while Stephaine unloaded and plated the food, was a blissful family moment I wouldn't have missed for the world.

The next day, it was cold and dreary, promising that a summer rain would be in before noon. I decided not to venture into the forest with the impending weather. Instead, I made my way across the little town to see the local historians. They were more than happy to help me find what I was looking for. Leonard Mills death certificate and where he was buried in the town cemetery, next to his little sister and mother who both died that winter of pneumonia. Further down, there was a photo of the family. I asked for a copy.

Before leaving the historians, I asked for as much information on the McGillan family as they could give me without spending the day in their archives reading. They were nice enough to give me a few pages that would give me a better understanding of who the family was. I thanked them both as I turned towards the door.

"You know that the youngest sibling of the McGillian family is still alive." One of them said to me.

I turned back with a frown. "They must be in their eighties or nineties by now."

"Oh, I don't think she likes to talk about her age much, but she lives here in town. Actually, I believe she lives right next to you, Lucy Johnson is her name." The historian smiled at me politely.

"I don't think I have met her yet." I forced the smile as my stomach turned.

"I shouldn't be surprised by that dear." One of the other historians, an older lady said while looking at me over her glasses.

"And why is that?" I asked.

"Your grandma and she never got along. Most of the town tries to ignore or avoid her. She isn't a pleasant person now. Your grandmother though," She smiled brightly at me. "Everyone loved her. You remind me a lot of her when she was your age."

"Did you know my grandmother then?" I questioned from the door where I held the papers in a death grip.

"Of course. Your grandmother was from this town. She was a beauty in her youth. All the boys loved her, but she only had eyes for that one." The older lady smiled at me.

"I didn't know that. My grandpa and grandma met in another town before getting married and settling down. I just knew she had this cottage here and escaped when she could. I thought she loved nature was all." I could feel the panic rising, with every revelation.

"She did love nature. The McGillan girls teased her about it every day. It wasn't right for a girl to love nature so much, that's what they would say. Called her names not appropriate for who they were." One of the other historian's chimed in.

"What names?" I asked through a thick throat.

"Mostly they called her a witch. No one could keep plants alive like she could. She would bring plants back to life that others swore were dead." The first historian laughed a little before shaking her head. "She wasn't a witch, she just understood plants. Silly McGillan girls."

"Oh yes, silly girls. Well, thank you for all the information. I really appreciate it." I waved with my hand on the door.

"Anytime dear. Come back again." Both women waved to me as I closed the door.

Walking down the street, I was reading the pages they had given me when I ran into a wall. Well, less a wall and more a chest. I looked up to see Dean smiling down at me.

"Twice in two days. This must be a record for running into you." He grinned.

"Or you put a tracker on me and just know where I am at all times." I let my eyes go wide in horror.

"Damn. Ya found me out." I rolled my eyes at him before he turned to join me walking. "I see you went to see the history ladies."

"Historians, Dean, they are historians." I smiled despite what I had learned. "And yes I did. I wanted to know more."

"And what did they say?" Dean asked, as I flipped a page over.

"Short story, I'm crazy as hell." Dean barked out a

laugh before covering it with his hand and motioning for me to continue. "Well, for starters, Leonard Mills is well and truly dead. So, there is no way I am seeing him in the middle of the forest at an abandoned house." I stopped so suddenly that Dean bumped into me. "Everything seems to be connected to my grandma though, nothing to the family, just her."

"Because she was a witch." Dean said matter of factly.

I gave him the death stare this time and he raised his hands slowly in surrender. "She was not a witch. That is just what the McGillan girls called her and since they were wealthy, no one corrected them. Morons."

"What does that have to do with your grandma?" Dean asked, frowning.

"Old lady Johnson is the youngest of the McGillan girls. The only one alive, I would assume. Which is probably why she keeps claiming I'm a witch too. She thought my grandma was one, why wouldn't I be too. One of the historians said my grandma only had eyes for one guy, even though she was pretty enough to catch the eye of all the boys, but I got the feeling she didn't marry that guy, since she didn't meet my grandpa until she went to another city." I tapped the papers to my lips. "I'm missing something."

Dean pulled the papers from my hands causing me to look up. "You know, you could always just stop going to the house and maybe Leonard would put himself back to rest."

"Dean, he ate. Ghosts don't eat. They can't drink. That much I know, I looked it up." I snatched the papers back from him. "I think I have to go back."

"I'm coming with you then." Dean announced.

"Why?" I questioned. "What could you possibly do except scare off the ghost that might be there?"

"I'm the apocalypse team mate." He declared with his hands on his hips.

"What does that have to do with this?" I questioned feeling the smile threaten to break free.

"This could be the start of the apocalypse." He shrugged. "You never know. Better to have back up."

"It's because you think I'm crazy, isn't it?" I asked with my arms crossed.

"No, it's because I think you're hot and I'm going to make sure it isn't some asshole dressed up trying to win your trust, only to kill you and dispose of your body in the woods." He said it with such conviction I blinked at him a couple times. "Plus I kinda like you."

"Oh. Okay, I think you have some good points, you can come." I nodded once before starting towards my cottage.

We reached the cottage just as the sky opened and started to pour rain. I invited Dean inside and dropped the papers on the table. Staring at the downpour outside I crossed my arms over my chest, frustrated at the set back. We would have to wait till tomorrow and hope the rain cleared out overnight. Dean stepped up next to me and watched the rain fall for a while before he spoke.

"Tomorrow then?" He asked softly.

"Yeah, tomorrow." I looked at him before nodding towards the kitchen. "Can I entice you to stay for dinner? I won't burn down my house."

"Very funny smarty pants. Want me to start a fire?" He motioned to the fireplace as he closed the front door.

"Think you can do that without burning my house down?" I asked from the kitchen doorway.

"I will never live this down." He mumbled kneeling in front of the hearth.

"There will be no living with me now." I called back entering the kitchen.

"I'm sure we will manage." Dean was smiling at me when I looked back.

Those butterflies were making quite a few appearances in my mid section lately. I opened the door to the fridge and began to gather things to make dinner for us. From the living room I heard a moderate amount of cursing before a whoop of excitement. There would be no living with him if he couldn't start a fire better than that.

The next day was clear. Blue skies promised the rain was over and the birds that chirped in the trees said they hadn't been washed away. I stood on the porch drinking a cup of coffee as Dean walked up the walkway. I offered to let him stay the night, after an internal debate even I could see raging, he declined and borrowed my umbrella to walk home. The decline triggered different emotions in me, but mostly a bit of a deeper endearment towards him. He wasn't trying to take advantage of me. He held the rainbow umbrella out to me as he graced the first step.

"Coffee?" I offered, taking the umbrella from him.

"After the dinner you made last night, I expect your coffee to be the same quality." He said following me inside.

"I'm not a barista." I shrugged before glancing back at him.

"Ha, ha, ha. You have so many jokes." He folded his arms over his chest before rolling his eyes.

I filled a second cup for him before asking if he needed sugar or cream. He declined saying he wanted to taste the sludge before adding to it. I watched as he sipped from the steaming cup and he waved his hand back and forth in a so-so motion, even as he proceeded to drink more. Maybe I was a barista too. He leaned against the counter while letting his eyes roam around the kitchen, which allowed me to take him in. He wore jeans again, I was starting to think that was all he owned, with a black shirt and a pair of dark boots.

Absentmindedly I rubbed my bare foot against the back of my own jeans. I was wearing a dark purple top with my hair pulled up today. No makeup, because I wasn't trying to impress anyone, but I was starting to think I should have. Dean set the empty cup carefully in the sink after rinsing it out. I followed suit a few moments later before heading to the living room and putting my boots on.

"Ready?" I asked.

"Oh yeah. I am definitely ready." Dean said stepping onto the porch.

Locking the door behind us, we made our way to the path and started down it. The ground was softer because of the rain fall and our footprints could be seen behind us, no other ones in front of us. We reached the clearing quickly and I frowned at the sight of the house. It was darker still. I glanced at Dean and watched him survey the house.

"This place is in desperate need of a demo." Dean mumbled and I could have swore I heard a growl, from the direction of the house.

"It looks worse than the first day I was here. I thought maybe it was my imagination." I said quietly.

"How long till Leonard usually comes by?" He asked, walking towards the house.

I stopped him with a hand on his arm. "No, she doesn't like people coming close."

"She?" He asked.

"The house. When I first came, it didn't feel like this. I was able to go on the grounds, but now." I shivered involuntarily. "It feels angry. Leonard usually came around 11."

Dean glanced at me but didn't say anything and didn't move again. He glanced at his watch before sitting on the rocks I typically did. I couldn't sit down. I paced back and forth, feeling like a caged animal. Something that needed to break free and do something, anything other than wait. I glanced at my watch and realized I had been pacing for almost an hour. Turning I noticed Dean staring intently at the house.

"What's wrong?" I asked.

"You're right." He motioned to the house. "She is angry." Then he raised those blue eyes to me. "But she is angry with you for some reason."

"Yeah, I was worried about that." I sighed heavily. "But what could I have done?"

Dean looked at his watch again. "After 11 and no Leonard. Maybe he is a no show?"

I shook my head. "In the months I've been coming here," I held up a finger when I heard a small sound from him. "Not a word from you. In the months I have been coming here, he has never missed a day." I took a step towards the house. "Something isn't right."

As if the words triggered something, the house seemed to grow darker and a scream echoed from within the house. A man's scream, one of sheer terror and pain.

I was moving before Dean could stop me. I sprinted across the short distance to the wall and didn't stop when I normally would. I rounded the corner and felt the weight of that choice hit me. The heavy feeling was the same feeling that I had in my own house. It didn't stop me, I pushed through with Dean calling my name from behind me. I reached the front door and shoved the broken door aside.

I stepped into the hallway and stopped. Everything was broken and run down. The house had been abandoned in a hurry. Furniture still dotted spaces in the hall and a room to the left, a sitting room I would assume, but the vines of the forest were reclaiming it. I felt rather than heard Dean stop behind me. The scream pulled at my heart and drew my eyes up the stairs. I sprinted up the stairs, once polished to show the beautiful marble that was now hidden under the buildup of time.

Topping the stairs I stopped again. Hallways split off to each side and straight back. The house felt heavy around me, Dean felt it too because he touched my arm gently. I pulled away just as gently. There was no leaving for me yet. I started down the hall in front of me and pushed open the first closed door, then the next and the next, until I came to the last door. On the floor in the room, Leonard was curled in a ball clutching his stomach. Only Dean's strong fingers stopped me from running to him.

What stepped around the door would have stopped me as well. She was dead, most definitely. Flesh hung in tattered scraps to her bones. Her dress was dirty with what I could only assume was mold and graveyard dirt. She looked at me and even without lips I could tell she was sneering at me.

"Well, well, I told you she would come Leo, my love." The corpse hissed at Leonard who glanced up at me.

"Why would you come?" His face was contorted in pain.

"I heard you scream, I couldn't let someone hurt you." I responded.

"Oh, you see, she does love him." Another voice hissed from somewhere in the room.

The house around us shuttered with disapproval. I risked a glance around the room, letting myself feel Dean's fingers still on my arm above my elbow. I heard the unmistakable click of a safety being released, but so did the corpse before me.

"Bullets won't hurt us, sweetheart." She hissed over my shoulder.

"I wasn't worried about hurting you, just disassembling you a bit." He commented back and I was glad to hear his voice was steady.

"Tori, you shouldn't have come back." Leonard said with obvious effort. "They want you dead too."

"Dead too?" I questioned, before his hands hit the floor again and he vomited into the pail before him. My eyes flew to the corpse watching with obvious satisfaction. "You poisoned him?"

The head didn't turn back to me, it swiveled, like there was little control. "He was going to leave me. He wasn't going to marry me, he was going to run off with you!"

I blinked a few times before those missing pieces started to assemble in my head. My grandmother only had eyes for one boy, even if she married my grandpa. She kept the cottage here, just on the edge of town, with a path towards the house. Leonard's ease of talking to me, feeling comfortable with me. Never questioning things too much.

"You were in love with her." I whispered the words only to be met with a duo of hisses from inside the room and a louder groan from the house. "The house is only alive because I carry her blood. You think I am her. So it dragged you all from your graves to relive this day." I looked at Leonard who was holding the edges of the pail. "The day you poisoned him, the day you watched him die, so she couldn't have him."

The walls around me shuttered and I felt Dean's fingers tighten a bit. "Maybe try not to anger them more?"

"Yeah, no kidding." I whispered as the wall next to me

showed a new crack. "I'm not her. My grandma died this year."

"You lie!" The corpse before me snapped. "You are her. Come to steal my betrothed. While knowing I only had a short time left to live." She walked into the room before turning on me again and screaming. "You could have had him after I died! But now, I'm going to make you see how we killed him, so you couldn't have him at all."

The laughter, if you would call it that, echoed around the room and through the hall. The house absorbed the sound as if it was food. Leonard was slowly slumping over beside the pail. I shook off Dean's fingers and ran to him. Ignoring the hissing that sounded around me, I lifted Leonard so his head was on my lap, before looking up at the corpses standing over me.

"My grandmother was a witch, remember." I warned them. "Power only grows within its descendants. Would you like to see mine?"

There was a pause in their movements before they stepped back. I looked back to Leonard turning his face to look at me. His eyes rolled around before focusing on me at last. The house moaned and groaned around us, but I ignored it for the moment.

"Leonard, look at me." He blinked up at me, the poison obviously very well into his system during this point. "I am not my grandmother, we share the same name, Victoria, but if you did love her maybe seeing her face as you pass, will give you the peace you need to move on."

He shifted and behind me I felt Dean step closer. "I loved her with all of my soul. We were going to get married. You look just like her. That day you wore the dress, it was the dress she wore the last time we saw each other." I felt the lump form in my throat and swallowed it away as he kept talking. "She was my first and only love."

Dean gasped behind me and I risked a glance over my shoulder. The hisses that came from the corpses as they backed further into the darkened room and the shutters from the house told me that my eyes weren't playing a trick. I watched as a wispy silhouette took form, and the person that could have been my twin came forward and knelt beside me. I blinked back tears that had started to form.

"Hello, my little bird." She used my nickname, brushing young fingers across my cheek.

"Grandma." I didn't make it a question.

"So many questions, I know, but he's right. Your grandpa knew that he wasn't my first love but he was an amazing man I grew to love." She glanced down at Leonard who was staring at her. "Now, I can bring Leonard to the other side with me."

"I don't understand." I whispered, feeling the tears fall.

"And you may never understand, my little one." Her eyes darted behind us. "But I could be wrong about that as well." She looked down at Leonard. "They tortured him. They poisoned him slowly over the course of three months, once they found out about us. When there was enough poison in his system, they gave him a dose so strong it made him sick for hours, before he passed away."

I felt the anger vibrate through my body so strongly it made my teeth chattered. "They killed him, because he was in love with you, even though he didn't break off the engagement with her."

"Yes, but because you have found them and I followed you, I can take him across with me. Bring an end to the eternal torture they have subjected him to." She touched her hand to my cheek again. "Thank you, my little bird, for this last gift."

Her touch faded to wispy white as I watched her disappear before my eyes. Leonard was gone as well. The dark feeling of the house was not and it was stronger. Dean wrapped those strong fingers around my arm dragging me from the house as it groaned around us. Standing out front of the house, I could see the corpses standing in the window above.

"We aren't done here." I turned sharply looking at Dean. "I need to do one more thing."

"What is that? I can't believe what I just witnessed in that house." He gestured with a now empty hand.

"I need gasoline and matches." I stated.

"You can't be serious." He searched my face.

"I'm going to burn it down. You can either help, or you can leave and let me do it. Either way, this place is going up in flames." I turned from him and stalked from the grounds feeling the darkening feeling of the house reach for me.

When I came back with two gas cans and a box of matches, Dean was still standing by the wall waiting. He took one of the gas cans and circled the back side of the property making a line around it before cutting through the garden of horrors and meeting me back in the front. I stepped back from the front of the house before looking up at the corpses still staring at me. Their jaw bones working in silent screams. I lit the box of matches before tossing it over the wall.

The flames jumped quickly creating a blaze that I had to step back from. In the windows above, those same corpses screamed, mouths wide, looking like some horror movie villains.

"Give Satan my regards. I'm sure I'll be going to hell after this, and when I get there, I have more in store for you two." I yelled before turning away from the blaze.

The house was too deep in the forest to allow fire

trucks access to it from our town. It would burn the house out before they could get there and take the damned souls to hell where they belonged for their sins. Dean and I stored the gas cans back in the shed behind my house before calling the fire in to our local department. A simple walk through the woods and we saw the house in flames, must have been from the lightning strikes last night.

Dean and I sat on the steps of my cottage, glasses of whisky in hand now. I sipped mine staring at the gate at the end of my walkway. Dean set his empty glass down in front of his feet. We hadn't said a word since I dropped those matches.

"I think they deserved it." He said suddenly.

I looked at him before nodding. "Yeah, they did."

"More?" He tapped the glass in my hand.

"Yeah." I handed it to him as he rose from the step.

I folded my arms over my knees, listening to him quietly refill our glasses. The town before me was buzzing with the news of a fire behind my house. But the gate blocked them from walking through my yard and into the woods. It stopped the nosy neighbors from getting close. I heard the helicopter before I saw it. I glanced up before turning my eyes back to the townspeople milling around. That was nothing new to me. Two talking corpses and seeing my dead grandmother's ghost, those were new things to me.

Dean held the glass in front of me and I thanked him before taking it. "Still think I'm weird?"

"Yes." He responded without hesitation, which caused me to pause in my sip. "But, I think I like your weirdness." He lifted his own glass to his lips. "Plus, who's going to believe me if I tell them what happened?"

I tilted my glass in agreement with him. "Good point."

We sat in silence for a few more minutes, sipping the

good whiskey my grandma has hidden in the back of a cabinet. I set my empty glass beside me before scooting close to Dean. I wrapped my arm through his and leaned my head against his shoulder, loving the feel of the strength that radiated off him.

"You know, I've heard that relationships that are based on some form of trauma never work out." I looked up at him as he turned his head to look at me.

"Well, then we will have to base ours on food, whisky and non chick flicks." The grin he gave me warmed my stomach more than the whiskey did, and settled my heart in a way that hadn't happened since my grandma died.

Maybe she was right. Maybe there was a 'one' for me. I just had to leave the city, see a ghost, and commit a crime with him before I would accept it was possible.

About Evelyn Belle

Evelyn is a stay at home mom to four kids. When she isn't writing she is catching up on her favorite tv shows. Her obsessions run deep and when she decides she likes something she is all in. Loki, Supernatural, Harry Potter, just to name a few.

This is her sixth short story published. Her first was released December 2018 in the Deadly Night anthology with her co-writer, Jenee Robinson. Her first novella was released in July 2019, titled 'Song of the Seas', with the sequel coming out soon.

To keep in touch with her and follow her upcoming works, find her here:

www.facebook.com/groups/evelynscalltothedeep/

Made in the USA
Middletown, DE
30 March 2021